T0066846

PITCHING
on the
BLACK

DANIEL PUKSTAS

iUniverse LLC
Bloomington

PITCHING ON THE BLACK

Copyright © 2014 Daniel Pukstas.

All rights reserved. No part of this book may be used or reproduced by any means, graphic, electronic, or mechanical, including photocopying, recording, taping or by any information storage retrieval system without the written permission of the publisher except in the case of brief quotations embodied in critical articles and reviews.

This is a work of fiction. All of the characters, names, incidents, organizations, and dialogue in this novel are either the products of the author's imagination or are used fictitiously.

iUniverse books may be ordered through booksellers or by contacting:

iUniverse LLC
1663 Liberty Drive
Bloomington, IN 47403
www.iuniverse.com
1-800-Authors (1-800-288-4677)

Because of the dynamic nature of the Internet, any web addresses or links contained in this book may have changed since publication and may no longer be valid. The views expressed in this work are solely those of the author and do not necessarily reflect the views of the publisher, and the publisher hereby disclaims any responsibility for them.

Any people depicted in stock imagery provided by Thinkstock are models, and such images are being used for illustrative purposes only. Certain stock imagery © Thinkstock.

ISBN: 978-1-4917-2782-9 (sc)
ISBN: 978-1-4917-2783-6 (e)

Printed in the United States of America.

iUniverse rev. date: 03/12/2014

CONTENTS

FIREWORKS

As she prepared dinner on the barbeque at the Salisbury Beach campsite, Jennifer was particularly excited. The Fourth of July was one of her favorite holidays, but this one promised to be even more special. It had been a beautiful day with high temperatures in the low 80s, and this evening, she, her husband Harry, and her two children would bicycle to Salisbury Center to view a tremendous fireworks display at about 10 p.m. Like many others, Jennifer had a special affection for fireworks. It was hard for her to explain the attraction, but she would always mention the spectacular beauty of the displays, the music that often accompanied these displays in the modern era, and the loud bone-thumping bangs that were all part of the action, particularly the action at the end of the show. The final salvos that punctuated the grand finale shook her to her toes and gave her an experience like no other in her life.

As she sat down to enjoy the hamburgers, hot dogs, and potato salad she had made, Jen's mind fixed on one thing—the upcoming fireworks. She conversed with her family by telling them of all the details she had read about regarding tonight's performance. The fireworks were billed as the largest display ever to be set off in this area of the Massachusetts coast. The fireworks themselves were to be set off from a large barge about 500 yards from the Salisbury shore. The barge had been loaded in Boston and had been towed to Salisbury Center just yesterday. Besides the fireworks, the barge contained several large loudspeakers that would be placed on the shore to provide the music that would accompany the aerial and visual pyrotechnics. A crowd of about 20,000 was expected, and while some would find such a crowd in a small beach area to be unpleasant, Jen felt that the crowd and the feeling of togetherness only enhanced the total experience. The site of the show was less than two miles from the family campsite, so Jen and Harry decided that riding bicycles would be a good way to transport the family to the spectacular event. The road from the campground to Salisbury Center was straight and had a wide shoulder. Safety for the family would not be an issue, and by riding their bikes, Jen and Harry agreed that there would be little chance of them getting stuck in the long line of traffic that would surely occur at the end of the fireworks show.

At 8 p.m., almost tingling with expectation, Jen led her family's bicycle caravan off to Salisbury Center. In her backpack she had plenty of snacks to keep the family occupied until the show began, and Harry had an even larger pack filled with various beverages to wash down the goodies that Jen had brought. Melissa and Mark, age 8 and 6 respectively, brought up the rear. Their job was not to carry any burdens but to stay close to Mom and Dad. Both of the children were good bicycle riders, and although Harry looked back every five seconds or so, there was no worry about the children keeping up with the slow pace that Jen had set.

After selecting their viewing site and spreading out a large blanket, Jen and her family patiently waited for sunset to melt away to twilight and for twilight to morph into darkness. As the darkness deepened, Jen became more and more impatient. These were the hard minutes for her—the slow minutes when the dark night slowly transformed itself into a pitch-black void. Then there was always the matter of timing. Sometimes the shows went off slightly later than the announced time. Jen found these delays almost unendurable.

But now she was waiting, just waiting. Her patience had reached the point of almost perceptible agitation, and Harry began to stroke her arm. He had brought her to scores of these events, and he knew all the parts of Jen's impatience. All of a sudden the night was shattered by a tremendously loud bang. Like a rock shattering a bedroom window, the loud explosion startled everyone. It also startled and shattered Jen's agitation, for she knew it was a test rocket, a sign that the real show was about to begin.

When the show began, it did not disappoint. Apparently no expense had been spared in order to present the best fireworks possible. Instead of only one rocket going off at one time, multiple rockets went off time and time again. Rockets were exploding high in the sky and right above the surface of the sea. The music that accompanied the rockets was loud and engaging and always seemed to be timed just right as the rockets provided a percussive beat that was like nothing else on earth. Jen was mesmerized. Her eyes were as wide open as they could be, and she moaned with delight and screamed with pleasure as she eagerly viewed each new part of the display.

But Jen's response was not an isolated one. Nearly all of the 20,000 who were viewing the show were having a similar experience. The blast of each rocket drew a cheer, and the reaction of the audience was very similar to what one might hear at a college football game when the winning touchdown was scored through a long pass on the last play of the game. As the minutes went by, Jen's body began to quiver. Her nerves vibrated with anticipation of what was to come—the wonderful, magical, totally enthralling grand finale. As the crescendo of the last bangs began to hit a fever pitch and the music soared to its final climax, Jen's body began to rock back and forth. The crowd joined together in one great Wagnerian chorus of screams. Then, when nothing could be expected to increase the crescendo any further, a tremendous bang and the flash of bright light occurred that was more intense, more deafening, and more final as a statement than any fireworks in history.

On a small hill several miles from the fireworks site, Hussein Muhammad took off his sunglasses and placed his cell phone back into his pocket. The small nuclear device he had placed on the barge in Boston had detonated just has he had planned. He got into his car and drove off into the blackness.

A CONFESSION

Dave Sadowski peered through the dim light as he entered the basement chapel of St. Mary's Roman Catholic Church. It was the Wednesday of Holy Week, and he was joining his eighth grade classmates as Sister Elizabeth took the class to confession. Two confessionals stood at the back of the chapel, and it was clear from the light that shone from each one that a priest was inside ready to listen to the sins of the students and then to assign the appropriate penance.

As he assessed the lines that were forming up the aisles, Dave was upset with himself for his failure to get to the head of the line so that he could choose which priest would hear his sins. The line for Father Stone's confessional already had twelve students. Six of the students lined up for the left confessional booth, and six others lined up to be on the right side of Father Stone. Father Stone was notorious for the ease of the penances he demanded. As Dave stood in the chapel, he could hear Father Stone exclaim, "Good . . . . good . . . . very good."

Although it was difficult, if not impossible, to hear the students relate their sins to Father Stone, it was clearly impossible not to hear him respond in this very familiar way. No matter what the crime—missed morning prayers or serial killings—Father Stone would end his hearing of the litany of sins with that same optimistic valediction of "Good . . . . good . . . very good." Dave realized that if he listened closely, he could hear Father Stone administer the penance. Inevitably, it would be something like, "Two Our Fathers, two Hail Marys, and a good Glory Be." This was the confessor to get, Dave thought, if he wanted to share his shortcomings with another human being.

Because all of the students knew that Father Stone was an easy touch, his confessional line was always crowded. Father Knowles, on the other hand, had no such line. Father Knowles was a hard touch. He would listen carefully to the person making a confession and then

4

provide a lecture on the nature of the sins confessed as well as a program for future improvements. He would also investigate the sincerity of the repentance offered and mete out a penance that would underscore the seriousness of the imperfections. He had only two students in line.

This relative length of the line was not lost on Sister Elizabeth. As Dave and several others milled about at the end of the Father Stone's line, she immediately came over and ordered them to get in line for Father Knowles. Several of the students instantly moved upon her command, but Dave hesitated, hoping somehow he could remain in Father Stone's line once some of the other students had moved. However, Sister Elizabeth was having none of it. She got right next to Dave and walked him over to Father Knowles' confessional where he took his place as the fourth one in line.

Since Father Knowles had a lot to say to each of the penitents, Dave was going to have a good while to wait. Today, this was something that Dave wasn't relishing. Today, for the first time, Dave actually had a real sin to share with the priest. It was an embarrassing sin, a shameful sin, and Dave was feeling humiliated in having to tell it to anybody. However, this was his last chance to unburden the sin, a sin which might get close to being a mortal sin. Since it involved a violation of the Sixth Commandment, Dave was unsure whether his sin was a spiritual felony or just a misdemeanor. The Sixth Commandment forbade adultery, but it included all sins having to do with improper sexuality. Dave knew that to make a good confession he needed to disclose all of his sins, even bad ones. Once the slate had been wiped clean, he could then enjoy the holiness of the Easter season without guilt. Indeed, in the Catholic Church, receiving communion in the time between Easter and the Ascension was part of a person's Easter Duty—a time when Catholics were supposed to purify and partake of the gift of the body and the blood of Christ.

As Dave waited in line, he got more and more nervous about what he had to say. From Father Knowles' confessional, he could hear the rumblings of the priest's voice. Father Knowles commented on the sins revealed to him. As Dave looked at the students coming out of Father Knowles' confessional, he could see the strain and anxiety on each student's face. Their time in the confessional had been a draining experience. Off on the other side of the chapel, he could hear the repeated phrases of Father Stone. The students coming from that confessional seemed to move more briskly with their heads held higher, but Dave was not in line for that experience.

Aside from the sound of the priests, the chapel was indeed a good place for an examination of conscience. Sister Elizabeth tolerated no talking, so there was no conversational chatter from the students. The chapel was very dark, illuminated only by a few emergency lights and by the numerous red glows of the small candles arranged in rows before the statutes of the saints on either side of the chapel's altar. The smell of the burning beeswax was familiar, and it triggered in Dave an intense awareness that he was in a holy place different from the secular world of superficialities where he spent most of his time.

As he finally came to the first place in line, he began to tremble. He was so afraid of what would happen next. He was terrified of what Father Knowles would say to him. He also feared whether anyone else would hear his sin as he spoke it to the priest. Would he reveal his sin so loudly that the people standing in line would hear it? Would the penitent on the other side of the confessional be able to hear him? Would he say his sin too softly and have to repeat it and thus ensure that someone else other than Father Knowles would hear what his shame had been? What if Sister Elizabeth heard him reveal his embarrassing sexual sin? Would that change her opinion of him forever? Yet, as shameful as he thought his sin might be, he had to confess it. He could not omit this most important offense and hope to complete a good Easter Duty.

Then, it was his turn to take his place on the right side of Father Knowles' confessional. As he knelt and closed the door on the confessional booth, Dave felt totally alone and isolated. There was no light, only the glow of the sliding panel that Father Knowles would pull aside to hear Dave's confession. Since Dave was an altar boy, he had no doubt that Father Knowles would recognize his voice. The opaque plastic panel between priest and penitent might keep each from looking directly at each other, but the voices were very, very clear to each one. He could hear Father Knowles talking to one of his classmates, but the words were indistinct. Dave hoped that his words to Father Knowles would be just as indistinct to the student in the other booth. But as he listened and waited, he began to feel himself approaching the edge of sickness.

At last, Dave heard the panel on the other side of the confessional slide shut, and in a second Father Knowles slid the panel across Dave's side, and the penitent and the priest were ready to communicate. "Bless me, Father, for I have sinned," Dave began in the usual manner. He told Father Knowles that it had been four weeks since his last confession, and he began to list the numerous sins he had committed in the month that had intervened. These sins were all very minor—such items as missed morning prayers, disobedience to parents in small matters, and violations of various Lenten food prohibitions. Dave had no difficulty confessing these sins and, in fact, seemed almost happy to own them. These were the kinds of faults that anyone could have. Even a very, very decent person, after all, might miss morning prayers a time or two. The big sin, however, still had not been mentioned, and Dave knew he was running out of time.

Finally, the time had come to admit to the big sin. As he began to make his admission, his voice trembled, and he hoped that Father Knowles would not cross-examine him about the particulars. Dave wondered if he could stand the embarrassment if Father Knowles pressed him for the details of this sin of the flesh and offense against God. "Father," he said stammering, "uh . . . , I had . . . uh, an impure thought."

There he had said it! In his excitement Dave hoped that Father would simply administer the penance—probably a rosary—and tell Dave to make a good Act of Contrition.

Father Knowles asked Dave a question instead. "Did you entertain this thought?" Father asked. Shocked that he was asked such a question, Dave immediately said, "No, no!" Even as he said the words, he could feel a great cloud of guilt coming over him. He heard Father say some comments about fighting against impurity, but Dave's attention was not on Father's words but on his own lie. As he left the confessional booth, Dave was not even sure about the penance. He had to say ten of something and five of another, but he wasn't exactly sure. Tears were forming in his eyes as he sought out the altar rail to kneel and do his penance. He whispered the words of prayer by rote, but his thoughts focused on just one thing—he had lied in the confessional. Of course, he had entertained the thought. He entertained it as fully as an adolescent could entertain any thought, and he entertained it for a good, long time, perhaps ten to fifteen minutes. He wondered how he could share this shameful, sorry story of his impurity with anyone, but he knew he couldn't lie about it.

As the class exited the chapel and went back to the classroom, Dave could see that the other students were cheerful and that the confession experience had caused them no harm. Indeed, many of them looked as if they had been freed from something as a result of the process. Dave, however, felt no such elation. It had been nearly impossible for him to reveal that he had had a shameful, impure thought. Now, he had certainly added a mortal sin to his record of imperfection. His mother would expect him to go to communion on Easter. If he did, he would surely commit another mortal sin for coming to communion when a mortal sin was clearly on his soul.

When he got home after school, there was no one around. Dave put his books next to his bed and buried his head in his pillow. His sobbing took his immediate pain away but not his extended hopelessness. On Holy Thursday night while he listened to the passion, Dave, for the first time in his life, felt intense empathy for Judas Iscariot.

PITCH MEN

So far, this Friday evening had not lived up to my workday and work-week expectations. I had taken my wife Trudy out for dinner at Applebee's, and despite the fact that the food was tolerably good and the drink was very good, the staff had moved the meal along much too quickly. As a result, I found myself at 7:45 p.m. watching the last segment of a <u>Law and Order</u> episode and asking myself Peggy Lee's question, "Is that all there is to the circus?"

I had already seen the <u>Law and Order</u> episode—in fact I had seen this episode at least three times—so I picked up a copy of our hometown paper, a paper notorious for its brevity, and found myself reading ads for entertainment possibilities. Nothing seemed compelling until I saw a box in the lower right-hand corner of the page that said: "Join David tonight at the piano bar singing all the great songs of the past 40 years." That could be a lot of fun I thought, and would still allow me plenty of time to change. I left the den and asked Trudy if she wanted to join me in this activity, and she politely said no as she usually did. Within 40 minutes, I was driving to the Tender Trap Lounge looking forward to some good music, a few good drinks, and maybe a couple of laughs.

Once inside the bar, I took a seat next to the piano and ordered a bourbon. David was already loosening up and playing an upbeat version of "Born Free." He had a weathered face, graying hair, and the look of a man whose only exercise was playing the piano. He wasn't fat, but his flesh seemed to sag on his bones. If he were a piano, I would say he was in a severe need of tuning. When the song finished, I said, "Hi, Dave," and he returned my greeting with a polite smile.

At this point, David urged the dozen people at the bar to join him in singing his next song, a Sinatra favorite. I wasn't particularly pleased that he had chosen "My Way," a Sinatra standard that has become rather threadbare with overuse. Nonetheless, he asked us to join in, and so I did. David had a microphone, and so his voice was clearly discernible above the singing and mumbling that was going on in the bar.

I have a pretty nice voice, and even though I didn't love this particular song, I saw a chance to show off my talents, and so I did. David's voice was on pitch, and he had, as one would expect, a good sense of rhythm. However, there was a raspiness and worn quality in his voice that kept it from being attractive. He had, I believe, a professional voice but not a good voice. When the song ended, David thanked the audience and then said to me off microphone, "You have a nice voice." I accepted the literal words of the compliment, but I noticed that there seemed to be a lack of warmth in how he presented this compliment. There clearly was no enthusiasm behind the remark. In fact, there was not any smile or facial expression of kindness to accompany this small gesture of praise.

For his next selection, David announced to the audience that he would be playing an Elvis song. This immediately got a rise from the crowd, but the song he selected was an obscure song from one of Elvis' movies. The only one in the bar who knew the words to the song was David. When he finished, the audience—now spectators, and not participants—gave a polite round of applause. A small smile came over David's face, and he seemed pleased.

As the night wore on, I noticed that David never again asked the audience to join in. When he played a request or a familiar song, inevitably people would begin singing. However, David did nothing to encourage this participation. In addition, I noticed that after one of his breaks that the microphone volume seemed to have increased a bit. I had a few more bourbons and was beginning to feel somewhat impatient. I had come to the bar expecting to be singing along with perhaps 80 percent of the songs. However, David's choices continued to be somewhat esoteric. Although a few favorites were played along the way, the sense I got was that David wanted to hear himself sing and wanted the audience to listen.

After I had ordered what I believed was my fourth bourbon, I heard David say that he was going to play a Bobby Darin hit. Darin had always been one of my favorites, and I wondered which tune David had selected. As soon as I heard the first few measures, I knew that the song was "Mac the Knife." This was a song I knew very well, and with my fresh voice, I belted out the lyrics with gusto. Even though

David's rhythmical variations of the standard arrangement made it somewhat difficult, I made my entrances smoothly. As I sang, David moved closer and closer to the microphone so that his voice could maintain dominance. I couldn't hear anyone else in the bar singing, but David and I were both at a fairly high volume in what seemed a rough, but somehow entertaining, duet.

When the song ended, the audience provided a good round of applause, and I smiled and threw back the last of my drink. David thanked the audience and nodded toward them and then looked at me. His face had no smile, and his body language certainly suggested no friendliness. Coldly, he told me that he was surprised that I knew all the lyrics. I told him that I had sung the song many times. He didn't respond to this comment but turned his attention to his catalog of possible songs. From this point on, his selections no longer seemed esoteric; they seemed bizarre. Several of the selections were melodies of secondary Broadway show tunes. I knew none of the lyrics. After about a half hour and another bourbon, David took a request from a couple at a nearby table. Unfortunately for me, it was a country western song that I was not familiar with. David sang it confidently enough, and the requesters seemed appropriately pleased.

With no singing to do and no one to talk to, I had plenty of time to drink and to think. Bourbon is not a chemical composition that intensifies and sharpens the general thought process; however, it is an excellent stimulant for self-centered ruminations. As I reviewed the events of the evening and my growing disappointment about my experience over the last several hours, a thought finally struck me. David's purpose at the piano was not to facilitate participation; rather, it was to stifle it. In addition, for some reason he had an attitude towards me. That negative attitude must come from somewhere. Since I had hardly spoken to the man and every time I had spoken to him I had spoken politely, the only conclusion I could reach was that he saw me somehow as a threat. Well, I did have a better voice. But he could play the piano; I could only play the radio! Nonetheless, he didn't want any competition; he didn't want his voice shown up, and he had done everything in his power to make sure that he wasn't shown up.

As I thought about this, I began to get annoyed. Here I had come out of my house, spent several hours of my time, and paid out more than $30, so that someone could put me in my place! He had not done it through head-to-head competition; rather he had set up a situation where I couldn't compete. I hadn't come out for competition. I had come out to be entertained and, I guess, coddled as a customer. Instead of being coddled, I had been musically marginalized. David's selection of songs, his control of the microphone, and his tyranny over the rhythms with which a song could be sung all made it difficult for me to join in. Keeping me from joining in was exactly what David wanted.

In addition to heightening my sense of personal injury, bourbon also intensified my desire to do something about this injury. When I saw that David was about to take a break, I finished my drink, tipped the waitress, and walked over to him. "I've got a question to ask you, David," I remarked.

"What is it?"

"Is there something about me that was bothering you?"

"What do you mean?"

"I got the distinct impression that you were playing songs that very few people in the audience might know. I also got the impression that you aren't interested in having people join in the singing," I suggested.

"You must have imagined that," he said.

"No, I think you were worried about the competition of some of the customers—this customer in particular."

"Competition from you? You must be kidding."

"No, I think you felt threatened."

"Listen, I am a professional; only in your dreams could you think that you might be a better singer than I am."

"It is not my dream; it's your nightmare. I would like to prove it."

"How can we do that?" David asked.

"Well, we can't do it here. You control the piano, the microphone, the music selections, and the audience. How about a neutral site?"

"Okay. Where?"

"I saw in the paper as I was looking for something to do tonight that there will be a karaoke contest at the Foolish Fox down the street Wednesday night. We can both enter it. That will show who is the better singer. Even if one of us doesn't win, we certainly won't tie. The one who gets the higher place has the better voice."

I could see that David was not thrilled with this possibility, but he had been challenged. He knew if he didn't go along with my idea that he would implicitly be saying that I was the better singer.

"All right. I will see you Wednesday night at the Foolish Fox."

I called Trudy to give me a lift home. When I got outside, my head was swimming. The bourbon which had been rather slow in assaulting my brain cells had now arrived at full force. When Trudy picked me up, I explained to her how the night had turned out. She wasn't sure if it had been David's actions, my sensitivity, or the bourbon that had produced the challenge that was brewing for next Wednesday. She told me that it was probably a combination of all three. I told her I thought it was him, the bourbon, and my sensitivity in that order. Whatever it was, I told her, I was certainly going to have an exciting evening next week.

On Wednesday, I arrived at the Foolish Fox at about 8:45. The newspaper ads had said that karaoke would begin at nine o'clock, but like many other karaoke events that I've experienced, 9 p.m. was a very optimistic target time. There was a good crowd at the bar, and the karaoke started about 9:17. The rules for the contest were simple. There was a ten dollar entry fee. The winner of the contest would get 50 percent of the entry fees. The second place finisher would get 30 percent and the third place finisher would get 20 percent. There were three judges—the DJ, the owner of the bar, and one of the bartenders. Entries for the contest would close at ten p.m. and the best ten singers in the final round would be the finalists for a second song from which the winners would be determined.

I ordered a bourbon and looked around the bar. I did not see David. I looked through the song book and I picked out "Witchcraft," a Sinatra song, one I had sung numerous times and felt a great deal of confidence in. As I walked back from the bandstand, I saw David enter the bar. I walked over to him. I said to him, "I thought for a moment that you might not show up."

"The thought crossed my mind, but I think you insulted my professionalism, and I had to do something about it."

David took a seat at the other end of the bar and ordered a small glass of beer. I saw him bring his entry money and his song selection up to the bandstand, and I could feel my competitive juices flowing. When my turn came and I heard the familiar arrangement of "Witchcraft," I sang with confidence and energy.

It took about thirty minutes for David's name to come up, and he went up to the microphone with what I would consider to be a bit of a swagger. He had taken pains to dress in a way that made him look younger with none of the unsightly sagging I had witnessed the other night at the piano bar. His song selection was even more carefully crafted than his choice of clothing. He, too, picked a Sinatra song, and he picked one that would be difficult for someone to do who did not have a musical background. The song "I Get a Kick Out of You" starts with a lyrical recitation that must be kept on pitch. Anyone unfamiliar with the beginning of the song would certainly fall into tremendous pitch problems by the time the recognized melody began to play. Like me, David had chosen a song familiar, and so he only had to glance at the monitor once or twice to make sure that his timing with the arrangement was right on the mark. He did a good job. He was, after all, a professional. I still didn't like the raspiness of his voice, but the bar didn't seem to mind and gave him a good round of applause, a round of applause that sounded to me very similar to the ovation I had received. As he sat down at the other side of the bar, he saw me looking at him. He gave me a small nod and smiled just a little bit, letting me know that he thought he had done quite well.

When the names of the finalists were announced, we were both in the group that would continue. I was surprised that David had gotten as high as four. He was behind a couple of rhythm and blues singers, a head banging fanatic who had done a good job on a very raucous and difficult song, and a country western female who was so on target with the song she selected that I thought I was listening to the radio. I was not far behind David, in sixth place, but I was behind.

When my turn for the finals came, I decided to use a little psychological warfare against David. I selected Bobby Darin's "Mac the Knife" as my song. I thought the selection might bring his thoughts back to an unpleasant evening at the piano bar, but I also knew I sang this song quite well and could milk the song's very showy ending and perhaps gain me a place or two in the final standings. When my turn came, I gave it all I had. The song is always a karaoke show-stopper, and my attempt at it this evening was one of the best I had ever done.

David had only one singer to wait for before his turn. I could see that he was feeling a bit of pressure. He didn't look at me, but I knew that he was thinking of me. Finally, his turn came and he walked up to the microphone. His look was serious, and he didn't have on the smile that he had previously worn. Whether this would affect his singing or not, I couldn't tell.

When David started to sing, I was surprised by his song choice. He had selected the Kenny Rogers hit "Lady." This song could be a crowd pleaser, and it certainly would show his versatility in that it differed so much from the Sinatra song he had started with. However, there was nothing he could do about the raspiness in his voice. The range demands of the song are substantial, and at the higher notes David's raspiness almost sounded like he was cracking, although I knew this was just the nature of his voice. I wondered if the judges had heard him enough to be capable of making the same recognition. When he finished, he received a nice round of applause and sat down at the bar. He looked over at me but there was no nod. I didn't see a look of defeat on his face, but I didn't see a look of victory either.

After twenty-five minutes, all the other singers had finished. The judges were compiling the totals and getting ready to announce the winners. When the order of finalists was announced, neither David nor I were in the bottom five finalists. We obviously had done a good job and had been well received by the judges. Then came the naming of the fifth-place finisher. All I wanted was not to hear my name. The DJ exclaimed into the microphone, "and now our fifth place winner, please cheer for . . . David!"

I was tremendously relieved. My name did not appear in fourth place either. I had been the third place winner, and the power of "Mac the Knife" had again shown itself as I had moved up a number of places with that song. When I looked back over to the other side of the bar, David was gone. There had been no congratulations for the victor, no camaraderie as part of musical competition.

In fact, I never saw David again. The next time I noticed an ad for the piano bar, there was a new pianist in the photograph. A few weeks later a short notice appeared on the obituary page of our local newspaper. David's name was there, and the write up included the many musical accomplishments and positions he had achieved. The details of his life indicated some impressive schooling, but an inability to find a position in the first rank of musicians. He had shown lots of early promise, but it was a promise that was not to be fulfilled. The information about his death was sketchy. He had been found in a hotel room where his prescription drugs and a bottle of alcohol were also present. No other information was available.

As I brought the paper out to Trudy to show her the story, I felt pretty bad. I wondered if the little contest I had demanded to salve my ego had something to do with David's death. I could have lived without winning, but could he? Maybe I should have been a little more compassionate and a little less competitive. In any event, I haven't gone to a piano bar since.

THE CONTRARIAN

The untimely death of his wife of thirty-five years left Steven Richardson very unsettled for more than fourteen months. Fortunately, his teaching job at a local college had a routine to it that channeled his thoughts in much the same way as the Army Corp of Engineers can channel a river. When the period of mourning and readjustment had ended, Steven decided that his life needed new interests and new outlets. While his wife was alive, he had controlled some of the impulses and reactions he had to some of the nonsensical and foolish practices he saw around him. Now he decided he would become engaged with the process of dealing with the foolishness.

One place where the foolishness of the world was at high tide was the local news media. One station in particular seemed dedicated to making people feel like victims and creating a sense of helplessness that went against all forms of individual responsibility and achievement. Steven wondered how he could counter this. One day it struck him that it might be commercially viable for this television station to present another point of view. While this opposite view could not be viewed every day, it could be offered twice a week in a manner that was engaging, rational, conversational, and good-natured. The key was to keep the commentary from being mean-spirited. The accent would have to be on thought—critical thought to be sure, but thought that could be followed by the average mass of people who were watching the television news.

And so Steven created the character of Doctor Contrarian. Using the resources of some of the communication students on his campus, Steven prepared three sample segments of what he would offer. He took a news story that attempted to dramatize the hunger crisis in central New York and showed how the statistics were incredibly unreliable, and the services offered to those in the hungry category overlapped and were peppered with waste. As he reviewed the videos he would be sending, he was pleased with the persona he had developed. He was not angry and intimidating; he was charming, thoughtful, and likeable. After he sent the videos, he thought that in a couple of days he would call the manager of the television station and get his reaction in person. However, even before Steven could make his call, the station manager called him and asked to see him for a serious discussion of what Steven had put on the table.

Within a few weeks, Steven was on the air. It was only four minutes a week, but it was four uninterrupted minutes. Steven never could have tried this when his wife was alive; it would have made the family much too public. In the past, Steven had wondered whether, in fact, the family's life would have been too public if he were on television, and he had questioned his wife's judgment. After two weeks on the local news, Steven had no questions about his wife's judgment; she was absolutely right. Steven had triggered phone calls and emails to the station in numbers much higher than the station manager had anticipated. In terms of Steven's commentaries continuing, this was good news. Emails, letters, phone calls, all suggested that lots of people were watching what Steven had to say and were responding to it. There were, of course, many who did not like what he had to say, but there were just as many who sent letters of congratulations.

Steven wondered how protected his alter ego of Dr. Contrarian would keep him at home. He lived in another city about twenty-five miles from the television station. However, in the world of the internet, no one stays anonymous for long. Soon, it was widely known and publicized that Dr. Contrarian was none other than Dr. Steven Richardson of Cortland Valley College.

Now, telephone calls started to be received at home. Steven was surprised at how angry the people were when they called him. His different position from theirs shouldn't be a cause for hate, he mused. Pretty soon things got so bad that he stopped answering his land-line phone and screened the calls on his answering machine. Friends knew that to get to Steven quickly, they would have to use the cell phone.

In late December, Steven provided a rebuttal of a news story that shamelessly and emotionally underscored the plight of apartment dwellers who found themselves unable to pay their heating bills. The news story seemed to suggest that it was someone else's responsibility to give these people money for heating. As anyone who had watched Dr. Contrarian could have predicted, the good Doctor was not going to embrace this shift of responsibility. In a matter-of-fact style that suggested a world of common sense, Dr. Contrarian made the point to the television audience that people who could not afford to live in an apartment by themselves should not live by themselves. He further suggested that independent living was a reward for people with independent means.

Within minutes of these observations, Steven's answering machine worked non-stop for nearly two hours. He was shocked at the rage he heard in the voices of the people who called him. Luckily, just a few words let Steven know what the callers' position was. What was disturbing was the fact that for the first time the people calling him started to use words like "kill" in their messages. The emails that Steven received were even more frenzied than the phone calls. Because the emails were anonymous and extremely hard to trace, Steven found more threatening language here. What scared him most about the emails was that in an email, the speaker had time to consider what he was saying. While some emails were surely produced without any review of the message being transmitted, others certainly had been read over by the senders. Steven marveled at the kind of rage and insanity that was at work in the community.

As frightening as some of the messages were, Steven found the whole business of being Dr. Contrarian very stimulating. He liked the influence he was having on issues in the community; he liked the fact that people knew who he was, and he liked the fact that he was clarifying his own positions quite well, and so he continued.

When late spring came and the time for public school budgets arrived, Steven thought it was necessary at last to barbeque the sacred cow. He pointed out the terribly flawed budget process, the waste that was rampant in education, the fact that increased money went to the teachers and not really to the children, the poor structure of the voting process where people who worked for the school district and their families voted on the budget that provided their salaries, and, lastly, the terrible record of achievement that students were able to display in spite of the six-figure investment that had been made over the years for every student in the school district. Because of the complexity and importance of this issue on the local scene, Steven gave a number of presentations on his views with regard to the proposed school funding. People all over the viewing area were discussing what Steven had to say. Not surprisingly, when the school budget votes took place, nearly 75 percent went down to defeat.

Where these budgets were turned down, those who were financially hurt by the refusal of the voters to pay any more taxes sought someone upon whom they could vent their anger. Steven's face was in the center of the bull's-eye. Those who faced position cuts or smaller salary increases than they expected were vicious and clearly threatening in their comments to Steven. Different, too, was what was happening at Steven's college. The president of the college teaching union told Steven that the state union had contacted the college's local and told them to put a muzzle on this Steven Richardson character. Others confronted Steven in hallways, and the tires on his car were slashed. In no uncertain terms Steven was told to lay off and keep his mouth shut with regards to the second vote that would be taken on school budgets.

Steven, of course, would have none of this. He particularly disliked the structure of the second vote. The taxpayers and voters had been quite clear in the first vote that they did not wish the school budget to be increased. Why they had to win again in order to get this point across was something that always irritated Steven. To protect himself from vandalism on his car, Steven began taking public transportation to his college. He wrote some of the best presentations he had all year to confront the education establishment and the news stories that the establishment seemed to have written for the station.

When results of the second votes came in, Steven was pleased to see that half of the "no" votes were sustained the second time around. Never in the history of this region had such a clear message been given to this educational elite. The time had come to shape up the system and give both the children and the taxpayers a fair shake. Steven celebrated with a few friends and enjoyed the accolades that came his way.

As Steven went to sleep that night, it was with a great deal of satisfaction. Whether this satisfaction caused him to sleep more deeply than he did normally, no one could say. However, the fire investigators who visited his destroyed home noticed that the smoke alarms were indeed working. Either he did not hear the smoke alarms or was unable to take any action when he did hear them. In any event, Steven's role as Dr. Contrarian was over. No one replaced him.

THE GOOD SCOUT

Don Anderson stood up next to the tent he had just pitched and marveled at what he saw. Stretching before him were hundreds of pup tents. Here and there, large brown tents that would house the headquarters of the various adults who led the Boy Scouts of Hudson County could be seen, adding variety to the olive-drab triangles for two that had blossomed all over the parkland of Hudson County Park, which jutted out into Newark Bay. This was Don's first Camp-O-Ree, and he was filled with anticipation of what the weekend would bring.

Friday night brought a pretty nice barbeque with hot dogs and beans, and ice cream for dessert. After this, the various troops gathered around campfires to sing traditional camping songs and any other kind of music that the boys could be encouraged to produce to build that sense of camaraderie that is such an important part of a camping process. After these activities, the scouts all bedded down for the night, and Don was surprised by how well he slept.

Saturday morning and afternoon were filled with skills training. The morning focused on fire building, using both friction and flint methods. The afternoon was spent developing knot-tying skills. This was an area that Don particularly enjoyed, mainly because he was very good at it. The square knot, the clove hitch, the bowline, and sheepshank were all part of Don's repertoire. Another knot that he was particularly good at was the timber hitch—a very practical knot for securing something very, very tightly. After the training, a knot-tying contest took place. Each troop designated three boys to tie a particular knot. Both time and correctness were used to judge the results, and thanks to Don's skill, his troop—Troop 20 from the Knights of Columbus—earned a tie for second place among all the competitors. A nice silk banner was awarded to the troop for this achievement, and Don was very proud as he watched it being attached to the Troop's colors.

After the competition, the boys enjoyed a robust chicken barbeque. Potato and macaroni salads, a seemingly endless supply of rolls, potato chips, pickles, and cans of soft drinks were all made available. It was a fine meal at the end of a very fine day.

But the meal was not the end of the day's activities. A competition that involved the entire Camp-O-Ree was about to take place. This was a gigantic tug of war, pitting one end of the camp against the other end. Because more than five hundred people were going to be involved, the rope that was used for this tug of war had to be substantial, and the leaders brought out a rope that was used to secure freighters to docks. It was about two inches in diameter and was indeed very sturdy.

As the leaders summoned and encouraged everyone to participate in the tug of war, they were not very clear where one side would begin and the other side would end. As Don watched things develop, he thought that the northern side of the camp was getting a few more people than the southern side. Winning was fun, but if the northern side has 55 percent of the participants and the southern side only 45 percent, this did not seem fair.

Not wanting to be pulled over the line early on and fancying himself as something of an anchorman, Don drifted towards the most southern end of the rope. He was an average-size boy, but was very, very determined and could be quite stout and stubborn when he was involved in any sort of physical activity. In fact, during the fall, he was on a championship touch football team where he played on the line. Although he was much smaller than many of the linemen who opposed him, Don won quite a reputation for getting around these larger players and making the tackle touches that would end the play.

Now, as Don got to the end of the rope, he could hear other boys observing what he had already observed—that the other side had more people tugging on the rope than the southern side. "How can we beat their side when they have so many more people?" somebody asked. As he heard this question, Don noticed something that immediately germinated a possible solution to the problem the southern scouts were facing. He noticed a small but sturdy tree right near the end of the rope. It was gnarled, with a number of branches that were close to the ground, and Don estimated the tree to be about a hundred years old. As he was studying for the nature merit badge, he had seen pictures of trees just like this one with statistical information that indicated how old a tree of this sort might be and what it might look like.

"Hey, guys, what if we tied our end of our rope around the trunk of that tree?" Don asked. "If we gather around the rope and the trunk, the people on the other side are too far away to see exactly what is going on. If they pull and pull and pull and get nowhere, perhaps their spirit will break. If there are a few defectors who give up, then the sides will be matched and we will have a good chance to win."

"What kind of knot shall we use and who is going to tie this knot?" one of the boys asked. Don responded that a timber hitch would be great, and he would be glad to tie the knot since he was quite good at the timber hitch.

Don grabbed the end of the rope and tied it firmly around the trunk of the tree. He admired the timber hitch he had put together, and when he had secured it to his satisfaction, he asked the other boys to give it a pull. "Wow! That's some knot." the boys exclaimed. And so it was.

Don and the other boys camouflaged the tree and the knot with their bodies and the other boys ahead of them took their places on the rope line. The contest began, and it was clear indeed that there were more boys on the other side. They pulled and pulled, but they seemed to make no headway. Just as Don had thought, a few stopped pulling very hard and a few others just stood next to the rope. Clearly the momentum had shifted to the southern side, and Don and his friends pulled quickly and hard, beginning to move the larger group into the direction of the smaller southern group. Seeing they were being pulled to defeat, the northern boys rallied and got their defectors to get back on the rope line. They soon had tightened all the slack they had lost, and feeling they were in the midst of a rally, began pulling very hard. Don and his friends chuckled when they heard the other side cheer, for they knew in their hearts that the tree that backed them up would never yield. Suddenly, however, they heard a strange cracking sound. Soon Don and the others could feel their rope move in a northern direction. As he looked back, Don saw that the tree was rising out of the ground! Then Don heard the shouts from the northern side. They too had begun to perceive a movement, and they pulled even harder. Don thought he saw a few defectors on the southern side move over to the northern side. As he glanced behind him, he couldn't believe what he saw. A foot and a half of the tree's root system was now clearly exposed, and a hole was beginning to open up around the base of the tree.

The next thing that Don knew, the tree with its entire root system was out of the ground. All resistance on the southern side had collapsed, and the tree had already been moved about twenty feet. Now, the northern boys were running with their rope, and the tree was beginning to gather speed. As Don looked with horror the tree was carried right into the camp director's large brown tent. The tree undermined one pole, ran into a card table and threw all its piles of papers up into the air. The tent quickly became a covering for the tree, and papers and people and camp furniture were all being tossed about. Adult leaders yelled and shouted, but the shouts of three-hundred fifty boys successfully pulling a rope overwhelmed all of the noises. As Don and his companions saw the devastation that had been wrought, they all melted into the masses of scouts.

About ten minutes later, things had settled down. The tree covered by a tent had become an object of curiosity. Like the physical remains of any catastrophe, it had attracted numerous onlookers. Don was in that crowd of onlookers, somewhat nervous, yet hoping to discover through the conversation whether anyone knew about his role in the proceedings.

"Look at this darn timber hitch!" the leader exclaimed. "This was a really bad idea, but this is a really great timber hitch." Responding to the camp director's question of what the damage was, one of the other leaders replied that, surprisingly, there was only minor damage to the tent, and most of the papers had been picked up.

"We're a little worried about the tree, but if we get to work right now we can replant it. It is amazing that the boys pulled it up roots and all, but that is better than if the trunk had been cracked in half."

With that information, Don returned to Troop 20's campsite. At the campsite he met the troop leader. He asked Don how his day had been, "Well, I tied a couple of nice knots today."

Thinking about the second place that Don had gained for the troop, the leader said, "Yeah, you sure did, you sure did tie a couple of nice knots today, and we are very proud of you."

CLAWS

Richie Dradowski stared out of the window of his parent's second floor apartment and looked at the muddy arm of New York Bay that made its home about a half and mile from his. It was low tide now, and the exposed bottom appeared like black ooze—a stinking black ooze. However, the appearance of the bay did not depress Richie, for today, his mother, two of his siblings, and he would be traveling to this very bay to participate in one of Richie's favorite activities—crabbing. Richie knew—and he assumed most of the people in Bayonne knew it as well—that crabbing was best when the tide was coming in. The sight of the black mud, therefore, created within Richie a strong sense of excitement and anticipation. The only thing that saddened Richie was that his father Joe would not be able to join the family this morning. He had to work but had thoughtfully arranged a ride from a friend, so the family could use the car to get to the crabbing site. This car, a used six-passenger Pontiac, was perfect for a family of five at the end of the 1950s. Its front bench seat gave Mom good access to her youngest, and the large trunk could accommodate plenty of cargo including all of the crabbing gear they would need: scap net, lines, box traps, and, of course, all the food that made a crabbing expedition much more than just a water activity.

When Barb, Richie's mother, had loaded all the supplies into the trunk and all the children into the car, she began the ten-minute journey to the spot where she could rent a boat and set out on the water for what she hoped would be a very productive crabbing location.

Richie sat in the front seat and fiddled with the AM radio to find the rock-n-roll station that he knew both he and his mother would enjoy. Barb had a nice voice, and very often she and Richie would sing a duet of some of the current Top 40 hits. Richie's younger brother Sam sat in the back seat with his little sister Mary. Sam was a year younger than

Richie, and at eleven years of age Sam was just beginning a growth spurt. He was certainly looking forward to this spurt since at the present time he was a full head shorter than Richie. Mary was only four years old, and she could hardly contain herself as this was going to be her very first crabbing adventure. Children couldn't go crabbing unless they could follow specific directions, and Mary had shown over the last few months that she had reached this level of maturity.

The place that Barb would rent a boat and obtain bait was in an industrial area of Bayonne called "The Hook." This zone featured many industrial warehouses as well as an oil refinery and numerous oil storage tanks. It was nothing like the Jersey Shore or Coney Island. In fact, in addition to the highly industrial nature of the area, the city dump was located on the very road that Barb would take to get to her boat launch location.

After a few minutes on the main Hook Road, Barb turned the Pontiac onto a cinder road that ran alongside the dump. As was the case on most days, several fires were raging on the dump, and thick black smoke rose high into the sky. This smoke, primarily caused by burning rubber tires, was as consistent a presence on the Bayonne shoreline as the skyline of lower Manhattan which could be seen to the north. As the Pontiac slowly rolled past the fires, Richie studied the wide variety of items that covered the dump and fueled the fires. Abandoned couches, broken strollers and bicycles, beheaded dolls, tawdry carpeting, ripped bags of kitchen garbage and other kinds of waste, all waited their turn to be incinerated. Further on, Richie saw numerous abandoned appliances. Refrigerators with their doors wide open gasped out their last breath as they lay on their backs; cooking ranges with their doors hanging loosely and tentatively from their fronts seemed to cry for one more chance at usefulness.

Yet amidst the extensiveness of this man-made debris, Nature would not give up without a struggle. Richie was amazed that so much green could still find its way into this zone of fire and desolation. He pointed out to Barb all the weeds—big green weeds—that seemed to grow right out of the garbage. Many of these weeds reached a height of nearly five feet. Most startling of all was a ten-foot tree that somehow had escaped the fires long enough to attain a reasonable height even though its foliage was only slightly more than skimpy.

After a few more moments on the bumpy cinder road, Barb turned the Pontiac a little more toward the east where Richie's attention was captured by the tremendous equipment of the oil refinery that lay ahead. Giant storage tanks squatted on the horizon. Behind them, high oil refinery towers let loose five-foot tongues of flame that stretched into the sky. Richie had learned that these flames were the way the refinery got rid of waste gases from the refining process, and he marveled how these flames seemed to be eternal. Whether it was day or night, he could see them burning when he looked from the windows of the family apartment. Even in the brightest sunlight of a summer day, Richie could clearly see the flames, and at night their presence gave an almost religious quality to his views towards the east.

After going over a small rise in the cinder roadway, Richie at last could see the bay and some of the structures that surrounded it. In front of him were a number of small shacks on stilts—perhaps nine or ten. Made from leftover lumber, shingles, and other discarded construction materials, these shacks provided summer getaways for folks who wanted to be on the water but who did not want to make the two-hour journey down to the beaches of the Jersey Shore. Wooden staircases led up platforms on which the shacks would provide an eating area as well as a small bedroom and bathroom. The plumbing was as simple as it was shocking. The front stilts of the shacks were right on the water's edge. After using the toilet, a person would take a bucket that had a long rope attached to it, toss the bucket out of the front of the shack and into the water. Pulling this bucket of water up, the user of the toilet would then empty the bucket into the toilet. A long pipe ran out of the front of the shack over the water, and this is where the waste would flow until it dropped the eight or ten feet into the water of the bay. It was not the most sanitary of operations, although it was certainly efficient. Richie had enjoyed swimming near the shacks on very hot days until he figured out what was going on with those pipes coming from the shacks.

To the left of the shacks was a large beached barge. The barge had a large enclosed deck that covered almost its entire surface. A small walkway two and a half feet wide was left on the deck for movement around the barge. Butting up to this beached barge was another barge without an enclosure, and this barge was almost entirely on the water. This latter barge provided a pier of sorts for people who wanted to fish and crab from its farthest exposure to the water, and a small shelter had been built on the waterside edge so one could keep out of the sun or the rain. On the side of the enclosed barge were painted the words "Beansie's Boats." Although Richie at first thought it quite unusual for a business to thrive in this strange and remote location, he learned from listening to various conversations that Beansie's Boats was in fact a very thriving and profitable business and drew customers by a word of mouth from many streets in Bayonne.

After parking the car, Barb proceeded with the business of acquiring a boat and getting the bait she needed. The young man waited on her and selected one of the twenty-four boats that were nicely lined up just a few feet from shore. Once the boat was secured, Barb began the process of moving the gear, the food, and the children into the boat. When this was accomplished, she positioned herself on the central bench and began to row in the direction of the barge that would provide a platform for the day's crabbing.

This arm of New York Bay was home to many sea vessels. Where Barb was rowing, dozens of scuttled wooden vessels clung to the bottom. Most of the vessels were barges, some with covered decks and some with decks exposed, and there were also several abandoned tug boats. One in particular—quite a large one—provided an interesting diving platform for some of the teenagers who visited the area. As Barb rode by this particular tug, Richie remembered an extremely hot day when four or five young men were diving off the very top of the wheelhouse. The tug had settled at a little bit of an angle, so the divers didn't have to work too hard to avoid hitting the decking below them.

As Richie watched his mother row, he admired her strength. She was not a fragile woman, and he had seen her on many occasions carry two large grocery bags home from the grocery store even though the distance was over half a mile. Now she pulled with easy and fluid determination, and the rowboat moved smoothly over the calm sea.

After nearly a half-mile, Barb asked the two boys if they would like to row, and they quickly responded. Each boy took an oar. Richie was conscious of the fact that he was much larger than Sam. In addition to being a head taller, at 120 pounds, he was more than 30 pounds heavier than his younger brother. As a result he didn't throw himself into the rowing with full force the way that Sam did. In this way corrections in direction only had to occur every ten strokes.

After a few minutes, Barb had selected the covered barge they would use for the day. They tied up at the end of the barge that was lowest in the water. When high tide came in, water would be about six inches above the decking of this barge. But now they had a big step of perhaps two feet to get up on the barge. Barges were dangerous, so Barb made sure that Richie kept an eye on Mary. Under the enclosure was the hold of the barge, and this area was open and filled with water. A misstep inside the enclosure that could be caused by temporary vision loss when one came in from the sun into the darkness of the enclosure could be fatal. Once all the gear was on the barge, Barb set up a crabbing location for herself, Mary, and Sam at the front of the barge. Richie wanted to have his own location, so he encamped himself at the other end of the barge at the point where the barge was deepest into the mud and closest to the water.

As he set up his location, Richie was pleased by this opportunity to be independent. He had two box traps and two lines, his own scap net. Both the traps and the lines were amply supplied with the bait that was used in this region—small sardine-like fish called "killies" that seemed to be a favorite food of the scavenging Jersey blue crabs in this particular area.

Once he got set up, Richie had time to re-familiarize himself with the sights of this part of the bay. In addition to all the scuttled vessels that lay about, he loved to look over at the most important feature of the bay—the Bayonne Naval Base. About a mile away from him were docked numerous mothballed war ships. During his years of looking at them, he had seen battleships, cruisers, destroyers, and occasionally a small aircraft carrier. Today there were no carriers, but at least there were two cruisers as well as several destroyers. In spite of being mothballed, they could quickly become readied to defend the resources and people of America, although as Richie mused to himself, the shacks, the barges, and the dump didn't seem to be much to defend.

As Richie looked back to his hand lines, he quickly got excited as he noticed his line stretching and moving away from the barge. He was glad that he had convinced his mother to rent an additional scap net and also acquire a second peach basket, the place where crabs would be put if they were a legal size. He liked the fact that he could scap up a crab all by himself, holding a line with one hand and using the net with his right hand. One of the signs of maturity in the Drabrowski family was the ability to scap. Catching a crab was a fun process. The Jersey blue crab, sometimes called the Maryland blue crab, is a scavenger like the lobster. Its scours the bottom for dead sea creatures and processes them into what human beings consider a delicacy. When the crab is eating, it is not quickly distracted by subtle movements. As a result, Richie or any other crabber, can slowly pull the line up. When the crab is about a foot or so from the surface, a net at the end of a pole is used to capture the crab. The movement of the scapper has to be deliberate and skillful. When the scap net breaks the surface of the water, the crab is likely to realize what is going on and make an attempt to escape by letting go of its food. It will use its two flipper legs to get away as quickly as possible. The scapper who has the most success will be subtle with the nets entering the water and direct the net so that it is below the crab, anticipating his movement. Richie had learned to do this quite well, and in the Drabrowski family this was a real sign of mature development even more so then the development of underarm hair and an incipient beard.

After about an hour of crabbing, Richie had already scapped three crabs and tossed them into the basket. To be legal, the crabs had to be four and a half inches from point to point of their shells. Richie had a pocket comb which was just the right length, so from time to time he would measure a crab to see if it met the minimum requirement. Richie's box traps had also been quite prolific and had already captured four crabs. Now he was pulling up another line, and when he scapped, he felt glad that he caught the crab. However, this happiness soon turned to disappointment when he saw it was really just a small one, not even close to one that might qualify for inclusion in the peach basket. As happened on many occasions, it was difficult to get the crab out of the net, and Richie spent a good deal of time shaking the net over the deck to get the crab out. He liked to get the crab on the deck and then capture it by securing it in place with his foot and then grabbing the back flipper. In this way, he could toss the crab twenty-five yards or so from the boat and probably wouldn't have to go through the process of catching and re-catching the same crab. In this case, the two-inch crab he had caught was giving him quite a tussle, and it took quite a while to get this fellow out of the various strings of the net. When the crab finally hit the deck, Richie tried to get his foot on it so that he could grab the flipper. The crab, however, had other ideas and quickly scampered into a crevice in the side of the barge. It was amazing how the crabs could fit themselves in such small places. These spots were great defensive situations for the crab. With the back of his body and his shell in the crevice all that faced potential enemies were the two claws. Even a small crab could do quite a bit of damage to one's skin if one weren't careful. Richie spent a number of minutes trying to get the crab. He marveled at the courage of this little animal. Here he was at 120 pounds probably a thousand times bigger than this crab, yet the crab fought on as if he had an equal chance of winning the day.

Finding no success with his battle with the crab, Richie looked at his line and saw that other crabs would need to get his attention, so he left his small but courageous crab in the crevice. When he looked back in the crevice a few minutes later, the crab was gone. He hadn't heard it plop into the water, so he assumed that it had wandered off somewhere on the deck, perhaps into the interior of the barge's enclosure.

It got hot as noon approached, so Richie decided to get out of the sun. There was a slight roof overhang a few feet away and so he placed himself on the deck and in the shade. He noticed that the peach basket holding the captured crabs was in the sun, and he decided to immerse the crabs in the bay water—a process that should be done at least once an hour—and then to place a towel over the basket and put the crabs next to him in the shade. Since crabs needed to be alive when placed in the cooking pot, the process of keeping them alive was essential to enjoying the crabs as a meal later. As he sat in the shade, he heard Barb, Sam and Mary shouting exultantly over a large crab they had just caught. He smiled, knowing everyone in the family was having a great time.

He thought of going forward to see the exact size of this giant catch when he heard the sound of a motorboat heading in the direction of the barge. Standing in the shade, he peered around the corner of the barge to catch a glimpse of the boat that was approaching the family's barge. It was a small outboard and headed deliberately toward Barb and the children. As the boat tied up on the side of the barge away from the direction of Beansie's Boats, Richie kept out of sight while he surveyed who the operator of this motorboat might be. Visitors had never come to a barge where the family was crabbing; as a result, Richie was uncertain about what this visit might mean. The operator of the motorboat, as Richie observed, was about twenty years old. There was something scruffy about him, and Richie was sure that he had not seen him before. As the stranger stepped on the deck, Richie could see that he was about six feet tall with black hair and was wearing black jeans and a black tank top. Somewhat suspicious about the arrival of such a character—in all his years Richie had never seen this happen before—he decided to stay out of sight until it was clear what was going to occur. In the quiet of a warm noon on this calm day, Richie could hear the conversation at the front of the barge quite clearly even though the conversation was taking place more than 90 feet away.

"Lady, I am here to rob you," the young man said.

"You must be kidding," Barb responded, "We don't have much money."

"This knife I'm holding should tell you that I am not kidding at all," he threatened. "You must have some cash. It takes money to go crabbing—the boat, the bait, you know, and I am ready to bet that if you had money for that stuff, there is still more money in your purse."

The young thug ordered Barb and the children to move to the side of the barge and step into the enclosure. Richie was glad he had kept out of sight, for it was clear that the robber had no idea that Richie was on the barge.

"I don't have time to fool around with you," the unwanted visitor insisted. "Get me your purse wherever it is—I want the money and I want it now. You have a couple of nice kids here, lady; you wouldn't want anything to happen to them."

"Leave my kids alone, you bastard," Barb screamed.

Hearing what was going on, Richie moved carefully and quietly along the side of the barge. From the sound of the voices, he figured that in the enclosure Barb and his two siblings would be looking in his direction. He was hoping that the young man had his back to him. On his way Richie picked up a 2 x 2 that was about six feet long. There was plenty of wood lying about, but this seemed to be the size that he could use most effectively.

"C'mon, lady, I'm losing my patience," the young man shouted.

At this point Richie became visible to Barb and the children. He put his finger to his lips as a sign for everyone to keep quiet. He hoped that Mary and Sam wouldn't give him away. Barb knew that the children had to be quiet. "Don't be afraid, children, be strong and be quiet," Barb insisted.

Suddenly, Richie noticed something moving on the other side of the water-filled hold. It was a small crab with its two claws reaching high into the air as it scuttled along, and it was approaching the edge of the deck. Within a second it slipped over the side of the deck and splashed into the water in the hold. At this sound, the young man turned to see what had splashed in the water. Richie immediately took his square post and smashed it into the back of the young man's head as hard as he could. He threw the full force of his weight into the back of the man's skull just to the left of his right ear. As the wood hit bone, there was a crunching sound, and the man immediately dropped his knife and fell into the water-filled hold.

"Let's get out of here," Barb commanded. Within ten minutes she had supervised the children as they gathered everything that belonged to them and placed it all into their row boat. She then instructed Richie to toss the wooden post he had used as a weapon into the bay. Then, as they were about to leave, she told Richie to untie the robber's motorboat and let it drift. As they rowed back to Beansie's, Barb instructed the children over and over again never to mention to anyone except their father what had happened. At Beansie's she explained to the boy that handled the row boats that they had come back a little early because her stomach had begun to feel queasy. She said that it didn't matter much, however, because as he could see they had already caught over two dozen crabs. She noted that they were good, large ones and certainly would make a nice snack after the evening meal.

Once they were in the Pontiac and on their way home, Barb praised Richie and the children for how they behaved in the crisis. "You saved us, Richie; you really did," Barb exclaimed. "And you two in the back seat were really very brave. I am very proud of all of you."

When Joe came home, the family told the whole story of what had happened. Although he was angry that such a thing had occurred, Joe could not contain his pride for his family.

"I think you left it the best way you could," Joe said. "The motorboat was probably stolen, and someone will find it drifting around the bay and get it back to its rightful owner. There are lots of barges scuttled in the bay, and if nobody happens upon the body in the next couple of days or weeks, it probably will never be discovered."

With that, the family discussion about the incident ended, leaving the robber's body a subject of attention for corrupting seawater, the predatory mouths of small fish, and the insistent tearing of hungry, scavenging claws.

CAMPING ESCAPE

Herb Morton was satisfied and comfortable as he sipped his second cup of coffee in his eighteen-foot camping trailer on Site 48 in Burnet's Campground. This was the second time he had taken the trailer out this spring, and he was feeling pleased about his location and the quiet around him. It was the first week of June, and the weather had embraced summer conditions. Herb had arrived yesterday, a Monday morning, and he was looking forward to a few more days of good weather until he left in the middle of the morning on Friday. Herb didn't want to be in the campground on the weekend. That was when all the yahoos and all their children would come screeching into the campground with their yelling, their fights, their bicycles, and the general chaos that could make what might be an idyllic experience even worse than living in the city. Now, as he looked out his window, he could see that both of the sites around him were empty. Long may they stay that way, he thought!

This year, getting away from his regular home was very important to Herb. The noise in his neighborhood had been growing over the past few years, and the behavior of his neighbors had gotten worse and worse. Part of the cause was the scattering of student housing that had developed as his part of town became less desirable and houses were chopped up for student bedrooms and student apartments. In addition, many older citizens in the area had either left for nursing homes or simply died. The young people who came to buy some of these houses brought families with them and habits that did not seem to Herb, who was approaching his 64th birthday, to include the kind of respect and consideration for neighbors that had been a standard expectation in the past. Added to this was the fact that Herb was still mourning his wife Abbey. She was the one who had instigated the purchase of the trailer, but she had been dead for over two years. If it weren't for his participation in church activities and the continuation of his life-long obsession to find out information about the economy and politics, Herb certainly would have been a lost and morose individual. However, he had his interests, and they seemed to sustain him.

The worst thing about living in the city, even though it was a small city of only twenty-five thousand people, was the noise. In the summer lawnmowers would rumble all weekend. When one mower was finished, another mower would be started up. In addition, there were other noises beyond that of the mowers. Even in private conversation, many people talked as if they were speaking in stadiums to seventy thousand people or more. Herb wanted to go up to the talkers and suggest that a much lower voice would be appropriate and practical when the person one was speaking to was only three feet away. He thought about doing this, but he gave it up, feeling that people would soon think he was a weirdo for offering this kind of advice.

If the conversations were loud, the children were worse. They made all sorts of noise—yelling and screaming during their games, crying incessantly over small injuries, and, worst of all, making terrible rumbling noises on the sidewalks when they drove their Big Wheels up and down the street thousands of times each day. Now, as he sat on Site 48, Herb relished the moments he was spending in relative quiet.

In addition to deciding to camp midweek while school was still in session, Herb had also decided to stay in a private campground rather than in a public one. Herb had learned long ago that although the public campgrounds had lower fees, their standards for behavior and eviction were so minimal as to be non-existent. As a result, public campgrounds almost always attracted a nosier and less considerate crowd. Burnet's had the advantage of being expensive—quite expensive. Herb had water, electric, and sewer service at his site, and for this he was paying $39 a night. Burnet's was a wooded environment and had a pond, but it was not near any popular attractions. The state campground about ten miles away offered sites for $20. Herb was paying nearly double but was hoping that this money would buy him the kind of experience he really wanted. One final point in Burnet's favor was that it was a small campground. It contained only ninety-eight sites, and nearly all of these were temporary. Some private campgrounds offered what are called "permanent" sites. Herb had an aversion to these campgrounds. People with permanent sites tended to do things that made Herb uneasy. They planted little gardens and added inexpensive decks around their trailers. Often they would put up little fences. As Herb walked through these areas in other campgrounds, he felt that he was in a refugee camp rather than a recreational area. Burnet's was not like this. There were three permanent sites, but these were for members of the Burnet family. Finally, despite its size, Burnet's had a little store that, in campground terms, was relatively well stocked. The store was near the entrance to the camp, and so it also served as a convenience store for the local population. As a result, Herb had found that he could buy other meats than hotdogs if he wanted to. The prices would be more expensive than they would be in a big supermarket, but the convenience factor was undeniable.

After taking a walk at 11 o'clock, Herb came back to his RV, ate lunch, and decided to take a nap. As he closed his eyes, the various birds in the trees and the rushing of the wind against the trees formed a naptime melody that quickly put Herb to sleep.

He had been sleeping for about forty-five minutes when something that sounded like gunfire brought him back to consciousness. It wasn't gun fire; it was something worse. It was the slamming of four doors on a large van in rapid succession that forced him to sit upright in a matter of seconds. The slamming of car doors was what he feared most, for it brought with it the screaming, yelling, and inane conversation of children. Right there on Site 47, a couple with four children had just arrived with a pop-up trailer. "How could this be?" Herb wondered. "Why aren't these kids in school?"

As Herb looked between his blinds at the people next to him, he ascertained that the couple was in their early 30s. The woman was a jolly type about twenty-five pounds overweight already and well on her way to the fifty mark, Herb thought. The husband looked fit, but his face carried the air of someone who was tired, very tired of what he had to endure each and every day. The children were comprised of three boys and a girl. Two of the boys were nine and ten. The girl was about seven, and the youngest boy was a toddler, about two. Herb just sighed.

It wasn't that Herb had always disliked children. In fact, he and Abbey had two children of their own, a boy and a girl. These two had grown up to be professionals and were now living at opposite ends of the country. Yet, although they were Herb's children, now they were adults. Those who were on the campground next to Herb had a long way to go before they became adults. In addition, over the last twenty

"A chance!" Jim responded. "I think we are going to kick their asses."

"I don't know how I want it exactly," Robbie added. "I can't figure out if it would be better to beat those bastards by twenty-five or squeak by with a one point victory in triple overtime."

"I'm for whatever causes the most pain," Tom said. "Those jerks walk around the city all year long like God's gift to the world. I want to see them defeated, and I want to see them suffer."

"Amen," added Jim. "Those dolts at Northeastern are dumber than sea slugs. It's time the world came to know what a bunch of losers they are."

"Yeah," Billy chimed in, "and our team, they are the ones who can represent us and finally set things right in this stupid city."

The afternoon wore on, and everyone in Robbie's room concluded that the Eagles' basketball team was the perfect representative of the college. The most significant representative, it was noted, was the Eagles' leading scorer, Larry Wilson. Larry, a six-foot six-inch forward, was the third leading scorer in the nation and averaged twenty-five points per game. When he had the ball, the confidence of all the Eagles—those on the floor and in the stands—was at its highest. "If Larry's on his game—or half way on his game—then those jackasses at Northeastern don't have a chance," argued Tom.

"That's for damn sure," Billy added, and everyone nodded in agreement.

Tom continued to throw down his vodka and cranberry mixture. He liked this drink because it didn't taste alcoholic. The problem, as he had noted several times in the past, was that the drink was so smooth that it was difficult to slow down or make a note of how many drinks he had actually consumed. At bars, this was not as big a problem as it was in Robbie's room. A bar would usually pour about an ounce and a half of vodka into the mixture, but in Robbie's room, the heavy-handed Robbie would generally toss about twice that much vodka into each of Tom's drinks. By quarter to six, everyone in Robbie's room was more than legally intoxicated. However, all of the drinkers could still tell time, and they declared in unison that it was time to get ready to go.

For his part, Tom didn't have much to do. He ran to his room and threw some water on his face and combed his hair. He did this out of habit, not because he might meet an interesting female. Tonight was not

41

a night for female companionship; tonight was a night for the castration of the Northeastern Cougars. As a final element of his preparation, Tom grabbed his Eagles' sweatshirt. Bright crimson, the sweatshirt featured a large eagle on its front with the words "Ignatius College" written in bold letters underneath the eagle. With this shirt on, Tom would boldly and clearly signal his connection with the team that he knew was going to win.

At the arena, Tom and his friends took their customary seats. Everyone had season tickets, a luxury the students were able to afford because of a special student rate. While there had been some talk of sneaking booze into the arena, this idea had been quashed as detection might mean ejection from the arena. No one wanted to be thrown out from this game. As a result, everyone brought along their bogus IDs. From freshman year on, students spread the word that it was easy to get a beer at the arena with its large crowds and need for fast service. Many of the bartenders were volunteers, and their ability to detect fraudulent IDs was very low indeed. In addition, there was a partial extension of the alcohol policy that existed in the dorm. The arena was an extension of the campus, and therefore an extension of the lenient alcohol policy seemed to have been negotiated between the college authorities and the city police.

As the game began, there was the usual competitive intensity. However, it became clear to everyone that something was missing. Larry Wilson was not on the floor. Larry was in full uniform and had participated in pregame warm-ups. For some reason, however, he was not playing. There was no news about his status from the arena's announcer. Spectators conjectured that perhaps Wilson was injured, but no one who had watched the warm ups had seen anything unusual. "Why the hell isn't Wilson playing?" asked Tom. "What the hell is wrong with the coach? Why isn't he putting him in?"

In spite of Wilson's absence, the game wore on quite competitively. Neither team was able to build up more than a five point lead. At half time, the Eagles trailed by only two points. "Damn this coach," blared Jim.

"I just can't believe this!" Tom howled.

The second half passed before Tom like a dream. The vodkas and the beers had finally hit home. He knew that the game had gone into overtime, but he didn't realize that the Eagles had lost by a single point until he saw his buddies get up cursing and scowling and heading for the exit aisle. As they exited, Tom yelled at them, "I'm going to find out what the hell happened!"

Tom knew that after each game, there was always a reception in a small auditorium off the main floor of the arena. He wasn't going to accept what had happened. He was going to find out why the Eagles hadn't represented him fully, why the best player in the school hadn't been playing, why the reputation of everyone at the school had been allowed to fall into the mud. As he rounded the corner, he felt somewhat unsteady and a bit dizzy. His anger, however, was such that he moved purposefully toward the reception. He heard a few people say something to him, but he couldn't recognize their faces or understand their comments. Finally, he made it to the main door of the reception room.

As he looked into the room, Tom saw about a hundred people. He saw a number of nuns, a few priests from the school, alumni and their wives dressed in suits and dresses, and several dozen students. He, however, was looking for just one man—Coach Conroy.

Finally, he saw the coach. He was talking to two nuns and a couple in their thirties who had brought their twin daughters to the game. The girls were about seven years old. "What the f**k happened to Wilson?" Tom bellowed about thirty feet away from the coach. At this comment, the room fell silent and everyone looked in the direction of Tom. Just as he was about to repeat his question, Tom felt the room begin to spin and his legs begin to fail. As he crashed to the floor, the vomit which always followed a heavy bout of drinking began to thrust its way out of his throat.

When Tom awoke, he was in a hospital emergency room accompanied by a student EMT. "What happened?" Tom inquired. "Where am I?"

"You are in the hospital, Tom. You made quite a fool of yourself at the reception."

"But that damn Conroy didn't put Wilson into the game!" grumbled Tom.

"That's because Wilson violated the team rules," said the EMT. "Not in a small way, but in a very big way. Coach Conroy had no choice, and you will see in the papers tomorrow that Wilson accepted the punishment and apologized."

"But this game was to show how good we were, what we're made of," argued Tom.

"I believe it did, Tom. I believe it did."

NEIGHBORLY CONCERNS

Steve and Debbie were both excited as they pulled their 24-foot travel trailer into their campsite adjacent to Blue Lake. Site 47 was a large and level campsite with easy access to the water. Because of the size of the site, Steve had no problem backing the trailer into position. Within twenty minutes of their arrival, Steve and Debbie had the trailer level, the screen-house up, and lawn chairs placed nicely around the picnic table and in the screen house. They both commented that this site allowed them to set a world record for the time it took to pitch camp. Added to the ideal nature of the site was the fact that there were no campsites on the opposite side of the road. Mother Nature had been particularly parsimonious in doling out land along the lake as there was a steep, steep cliff that rose about seventy-five feet just on the other side of the camp road. To the north of their campsite, Debbie noticed an older couple who also had a travel trailer as well as a fairly well-behaved poodle. They appeared to be perfect neighbors for a quiet and relaxing vacation in the woods.

However, as Steve glanced south, his anxiety grew. This southern campsite was about fifteen yards from Site 47. It was separated from Steve and Debbie's site by some thick foliage, a number of trees, and a few boulders, but as Steve perused the site, he could see two cars, two adult-size pup tents and a large pop-up tent trailer. Steve didn't see anyone around. Nonetheless, he imagined that since it was several miles to the main swimming area, the people from this campsite might have another car or van which they had taken to the beach area.

"How many people are on Site 46?" Debbie asked.

"Well," responded Steve, "I would guess that if we allowed two people per pup tent and maybe as many as four in the big pop-up, there could be eight or perhaps nine people on that Site."

"Are they adults or kids?" inquired Debbie.

"That's a good question," Steve responded. "Since I don't see any evidence of bicycles—no bicycles on the site—and since I don't see any bicycle racks on the cars, I don't know if we do have children on Site 46."

"Then you think we have about eight adults next to us," Debbie said.

"Yeah, I wouldn't be surprised," Steve sighed.

"I hope we're wrong," Debbie added.

"Me too. You know these state campgrounds drive me crazy. They put out all these rules, but you and I are probably the only ones that follow them. The book of rules and regulations that we had been given at registration were also clearly posted on a board at the office. These rules said that there could be no more than four adults on any one campsite unless they were adult children who belonged to a family. Furthermore, there weren't supposed to be more than two cars on a site, nor was there supposed to be more than one tent when a wheeled recreation vehicle of any sort was on the site. I am beginning to think that these folks might have set a record for breaking campground regulations," Steve concluded.

"Yes," Debbie sadly said, "the rules are just for us."

"I sure do wonder where they are," Steve remarked.

"Oh, they could be at the beach, or at that big water park that we saw about ten miles from here, or they could be seeing some of the sights that are in this area. There are plenty of places of interest. Or, I fear to say this," Debbie said, "they might be out there shopping for party supplies. Eight adults and a large quantity of alcohol might put a damper on the tranquil experience we wanted to have."

Such speculations continued over the next couple of hours, but they diminished as Debbie and Steve launched their kayaks into the lake. They both loved to paddle, and this day was particularly beautiful. Their exertions build up their appetites and served to increase their anticipation of their first camping meal, a barbequed treat that they both looked forward to.

After the kayaking, Steve asked Debbie if she was ready for a glass of wine. One of Steve's great pleasures was sitting around a charcoal fire that was turning from black to gray as he sipped a good but inexpensive Cabernet.

"Oh, I just hope our neighbors aren't getting pie-eyed at some gin mill," Steve interjected. "The thought of an octet of inebriated and inconsiderate individuals stresses me out a little bit, and I have awful flashbacks of some of the yo-yos we have run into in the past."

"Well, let's be optimistic; perhaps these people will be ideal campers," Debbie suggested. "Right now, we just don't know."

After supper, Steve grabbed his fishing gear and waded out into the lake. He wasn't much of a fisherman, but he liked to play around with a bobber, a hook, and a worm and see if he could entice some of the small fish who lived near the shore into a little contest of skill. This evening, Steve found the conditions almost perfect. The wind was coming gently from a north-northwesterly direction, and it was gently easing Steve's bobber away from the shore and towards deeper water. He didn't have to cast very far, and the slight breeze would carry the bobber and its passenger out into water where some fish might be looking for something to eat.

As the light faded, Steve finished his fishing and returned to the campsite where Debbie informed him that their northern neighbors had retired for the evening.

"But where are the southern folks?" wondered Steve.

"Maybe they have gone to a nearby resort," Debbie suggested. "Sometimes people like to use their campground as a base and head off for other sites. We don't know how big the missing vehicle is. Perhaps it could accommodate all eight or nine of them. I've also heard that there are people who set up a campsite and go back to their homes in the city for a couple of days of work and then return."

"If that's so, it would be great for us," Steve concluded. "I've had a chance to look at the two cars that are left, and one of them has a hitch. I wonder if they pulled the pop-up with that vehicle or if the larger van we have imagined also has a hitch."

The next day, Steve and Debbie did more kayaking, more fishing, and even enjoyed some swimming at the very nice beach that was part of the state campground. Coming back to their site in the late afternoon, there still was no sign of life at Site 46. The day had definitely gotten warmer, and the breeze that had been blowing from a northerly direction now turned to one blowing from the south.

At supper time the older woman from the northern campsite came over with several pieces of pie for Steve and Debbie to sample. When Steve asked her whether she had ever seen the inhabitants of Site 46, she commented that she and her husband had arrived a day before Steve and Debbie, but she had not seen anybody at Site 46. She said that it had looked then just as it looked now. Steve remarked that sometimes it was difficult to figure people out, and after they all laughed at this observation, the older woman said that it was time to walk her poodle.

After a great night's sleep—one of the quietest nights they had ever experienced in a public campground—Steve and Debbie awoke to the smell of bacon. The older couple in the campsite to the north of them loved to have bacon and eggs each morning, and they loved to have their breakfast at precisely 7 a.m. This was fine with Steve, for he already had eight good hours of sleep.

As the smell of bacon dissipated and the sun rose higher and hotter in the sky on this unusually calm day, Steve began to notice something. At first he wasn't sure what the sensation was. However, in a little while he began to notice that a different smell was beginning to penetrate his nostrils. He wasn't sure exactly what it was, but he was sure that he had smelled something like it before. He looked under his trailer to see if he could find a possible cause, but there was nothing. Then he looked around the campsite to see if some garbage had been picked up by an animal and left at the site. He found nothing, but the scent kept getting stronger. Then he remembered when he and Debbie had once gone on vacation that a chipmunk had gotten trapped in the garage and had died. He walked around the perimeter of the campsite to see if he could spot a dead animal, perhaps one that had been killed by a predator and then left behind. He saw no animals, but he did notice that the smell got stronger as he got closer to Site 46.

"I'm going to go over to Site 46 and poke around a little bit," Steve said.

"Go ahead," advised Debbie. "I don't see what the harm would be."

As Steve walked onto Site 46, the smell became intense. Walking near the pop-up, he could see that all the shades and curtains were drawn. He went over to the door of the camper and knocked, but as he expected, there was no answer. Then he tried the door knob, but the camper was locked. Then he walked over to the pup tents. The smell was really noticeable. It was a very unpleasant smell. Breathing through his mouth, so he wouldn't have to smell the horrible odor, Steve unzipped one of the tents. Once he pulled back the flap, he nearly vomited. Lying before him were two decaying bodies, each with bloody wounds to the head.

"Christ, Debbie!" Steve screamed. "Run down to the office; tell them to call the state police. A terrible crime has been committed here."

When the police arrived, they found that the other tent also contained two bodies. The pop-up camper contained an additional three. All of the victims had been killed gangland style. They had bullet holes in the backs of their heads. In relative quiet the investigating police were looking and examining the crime that was before them. Soon the bodies of the neighbors that Steve and Debbie had never met were being placed into large plastic bags and then in ambulances.

ANTLERS

Bobby Nichols glanced out of his living room window into the pre-dawn darkness as he sipped a cup of coffee. He could clearly make out the outline of his Uncle Ray's house about 100 yards from his across the road in this rural part of Central New York. Uncle Ray's house, like Bobby's, was a modest home and a quite typical purchase for someone who is a member of the upper lower class. The clapboard siding on Uncle Ray's house could have used a coat of paint, and the roof with a few sections of moss growing upon it had about five good years left on it. The house was close to the road, and the short cement sidewalk that lead up to it was cracked and had heaved in several places as a result of a long winter.

Bobby's house was in a similar state of disrepair but was a bit smaller, having one less bedroom. However, Bobby did not need more than the two bedrooms. Like his Uncle Ray, Bobby lived alone. The fact that he lived in a house at all was not something that Bobby had planned. Uncle Ray had purchased the house that Bobby lived in for $32,000, about $18,000 less than the purchase price of his own home. Bobby was in his late twenties and had been bouncing around from residence to residence as he moved from one construction or restaurant job to another. Sometimes in the past when things were tough, Bobby would take up residence for several months at the houses and apartments of some of his friends. These extended couch encampments would inevitably end in a drunken night when Bobby was asked to find other accommodations as quickly as possible. Uncle Ray was a hard man, but somewhere in the granite quarry of his heart was a soft spot for family. Bobby was Uncle Ray's only nephew, and setting him up in his own house struck Uncle Ray as a fitting tribute to his late sister.

While Uncle Ray felt some consolation and some pride in setting Bobby up in a house, Bobby had begun to feel a sense of diminishing returns from this gift of an accommodation. Whenever he was with his uncle, Bobby had the sense that Uncle Ray felt that Bobby owed him something—an undefined but increasingly large kind of something. It was something that was larger than gratitude, more than obedience, greater than obligation. It was as if Uncle Ray had saved Bobby's life, not once but three or four times. There was also this smugness that Uncle Ray had about his views on life. Since he was the provider and Bobby was the receiver, Uncle Ray concluded that he knew what life was like and how to succeed in it. Bobby, of course, was not a success; he was the loser. Uncle Ray was now fifty-five years old and throughout his life he had been both fortunate and focused. Although he had neither great talent nor much of an education, he had the good sense to get a factory job, show up every day, and be disciplined enough to keep on working. After thirty years, he had made a decent wage, and when his plant shut down, Uncle Ray was in line to get one of the highest severance packages that the closing plant offered. He had also taken advantage of the retirement plan that his work place offered and was disciplined enough to invest funds in this plan at various local banks when the interest rates were much higher. With no descendants, Uncle Ray was in a position to lead a decent, if not an extravagant, and exciting life.

Bobby, on the other hand, was just scratching by. When he was able, he gave Uncle Ray $200 a month as part of a long-term repurchase plan on the house. Uncle Ray did not charge any interest on this purchasing plan. His attitude was that if Bobby paid anything it was all money on the plus side of the plan. He also thought that the $200 a month payment would give Bobby a sense of pride. During some months Bobby found it easy to come up with the $200; in other months Bobby's employment might barely earn the $200. In those months, expenses for food and utilities left Bobby with just about nothing and there were months—sometimes several months—when Bobby made no payment to Uncle Ray at all. With their homes in such close proximity, it was very easy for Uncle Ray to admonish Bobby when Bobby got behind in his payments. During these times, the sense of pride and accomplishment that Uncle Ray had desired to instill in Bobby often turned to a sense of shame and failure. Beyond money matters, Uncle Ray was always quick to offer advice to Bobby on how Bobby should be living his life. Here his smugness became particularly annoying for Bobby. He could take, with some grains of salt, his Uncle Ray's haranguing of him on financial matters. However, when Uncle Ray would make pronouncements from his high horse on matters of romance, friends, and sports—issues that were very important to a young man in his twenties—Bobby would find such advice and opinions intolerable.

Yet, here he was, dependent on Uncle Ray for the place in which he lived and tied to him exclusively as the only family member in the vicinity.

Today, Bobby and Uncle Ray had agreed to go deer hunting. This was an activity that both men enjoyed, and both of them found some success in it. In fact, each year both men were able to score at least one deer, and sometimes they were able to take two or three apiece. Last year Bobby bagged a particularly large doe that provided him with meat for several months and helped him to extend his meager budget. Uncle Ray, on the other hand, had to wait a little longer last year to make a kill, but when he did, it was very worthwhile. Right at the end of the season he got a large trophy buck, and the antlers of this fine animal occupied a place of honor in Uncle Ray's living room. Unfortunately, Uncle Ray's success lead to a whole series of pronouncements of what one should do to find the best targets during the hunting season. Bobby, of course, was the audience for these lectures. When Bobby protested that luck had a lot to do with his successful hunt, Uncle Ray became incensed and proceeded to unload a catalog of arguments about how the good hunter would do all sorts of things not only to ensure that he would get a deer but that he would get one of the finest deer around. When Bobby countered that when Uncle Ray had used all of these same techniques the four or five times they had gone out previously and had come up empty, Uncle Ray responded that it was such ignorance on Bobby's part about the process of hunting that kept him from being as fine a hunter as his uncle was.

When Bobby and Ray hunted, neither one would wear any of the recommended bright colors that helped hunters from shooting each other. Instead of bright oranges, the men wore camouflage suits. As an older hunter, Ray felt that he had the right to wear camouflage, and he informed Bobby that only a sissy would wear the recommended orange. Since Bobby spent a lot of his time in the Army and Navy surplus stores buying camouflage clothing among other things, this advice on what one should wear on the hunt was one piece of advice that he easily accepted.

Just as he was about finished with his coffee, Bobby heard Ray's truck pull into his driveway. He quickly gathered his gear and grabbed his gun as he went out the door to join Ray for what he hoped would be a successful hunt. Once Bobby settled in the truck, Ray began to berate him about the fact that he had not applied camouflage paint to his face. "The damn deer will see you two-hundred yards off!" Ray exclaimed. "And another thing," Ray added. "What did you do with that special fragrance that I gave to you? You want to smell like an animal, not like a powdered and showered human being. If the wind picks up your scent, we'll have no chance of getting a deer today." Bobby just grunted a response and hoped that for the rest of the trip Ray would just shut up.

When they got to their favorite hunting site, Ray told Bobby what the plan would be for this morning's hunt. "Bobby, you get up on the side of the hill over there that overlooks this ravine that runs to the northwest. The deer like to come through here later in the morning. When they do, you get behind them. I'll be in that stand of trees down there to the south, waiting for the deer to come. I'll check out what's there and take a shot at the biggest one. If the deer hear me and come back your way, that's your chance; don't blow it!"

Bobby did as he was told and after about an hour, he could hear some movement in the woods to his right. He held his breath, and about fifty yards away three does and a large buck could be seen zigzagging in and out of some of the trees at the bottom of the ravine. He didn't have a clear shot at them, and he took Ray's commands to force the deer towards Ray. He circled behind them and made a little noise and they went on a track right towards Ray. If Ray missed and the deer ran back in his direction, Bobby thought he would have a clear shot at the buck. As the deer got closer, Bobby could see Ray move just a bit from behind a tree. Bobby could see Ray clearly, but the deer were stilled screened from a full view of Ray by the trunk of a tree.

As he waited for Ray to fire, Bobby thought how intolerable Ray would be if he killed the big buck that was with this group. Bobby wouldn't hear the end of it for weeks. Even if Bobby did get a deer himself in the next few weeks, it probably wouldn't be as big as this buck. He would hear about Ray's skills and his own inadequacies over and over and over again. When he saw Ray lift his gun to shoot, Bobby lifted his own gun and when he had secured his target, he fired. When the shot rang out, the deer sprinted off with amazing speed. Bobby took a deep breath and sat on the ground. He was sure he had hit his target.

At the inquest, the officials ruled that the shooting had been accidental. Bobby was admonished for wearing camouflage clothing in the woods, but he explained that he was just doing what his uncle wanted him to do. As the bureaucratic processes of Ray's death eventually unfolded, Bobby found out that he was listed as the sole heir of Uncle Ray's estate. After a few months, he moved into Ray's place. The first thing he did to remodel the new dwelling was to pry off the antlers that Ray had so proudly mounted and throw them in the garbage.

CROSSED COUNTRY

February 17th gifted central New York with one of the most magnificent days of what had been a long winter season. After being dropped off at his home, Richard Stevenson could feel the beauty of the day as a warming sun caressed his left cheek, and cold but calm air greeted his ungloved hands. Although he was 98 percent blind, Richard still tried to maintain his fitness. This was a day to get outside, he mused; I hope Mindy is home to join me in some outdoor activity.

However, as Richard opened the garage door and thrust out his cane, he was quickly disappointed; the family sedan was gone. Still, he was not totally defeated.

"I don't know," he said to himself. "I think I could do some cross country skiing by myself. I know how to ski, and the terrain around here is somewhat familiar to me. Yeah, I wanna be independent. I can't wait around for Mindy to be here to do the manly things I want to do."

Certain of his decision, Richard entered the house and quickly put on his skiing clothes. He searched around in the hall closet and miraculously found both his ski boots and his ski gloves. *The Gods are certainly smiling on me today,* he thought.

After some difficulty, he located the skis that would fit his boots and the poles that he could comfortably use. He left his cane inside the garage and ventured out onto the driveway where it took him nearly ten minutes to get his skis on. Standing ready with poles in hand, he thought about his route. First, he would have to get over the banks of snow that the plow had created. Then he would have to choose a route that he could follow. Richard knew that the family motor home was parked for the season northwest of the garage door. If he could touch the bumper of the motor home and then turn directly west, he would be able to traverse much of the back yard. It would be nearly sixty yards to the fir trees he had planted about four years ago. He would turn south at this point and ski for about thirty yards. Then, hitting another row of trees, he could ski back toward his house for about fifty yards until he would come close to the utility barn and the deck that projected from the rear of his house. This would be the downhill portion of his circuit, and he already felt a bit excited about the speed he would pick up on his slide downhill.

With this plan in mind, Richard crossed the snow bank. He had to put tremendous pressure on his poles, and he could feel them bending beneath his weight and force. Once over the bank, he tried to remember the basics of cross country skiing. He slid along okay, but it was work. *Where is the darn motor home?* he asked himself. He swung his ski pole around him in a circle, but there was no motor home. *Did I just miss it?* he wondered. *It must be close by,* he thought.

In any event he knew that he wanted to ski and not to look for a twenty-foot long landmark, so he headed in the direction he thought was west to begin his trip towards the fir trees. After about twenty-five yards he hit a bumpy stretch of earth that he couldn't place clearly on his property. *I guess I'm closer to the trees on the right than I thought,* he told himself. Based on this conclusion, he kept moving forward. After forty more yards, he stopped again. The terrain was flat, but he had no idea exactly where he was. His home was between two other residences, one of which was about two hundred yards from his garage. Farmland surrounded the back portion of his property. He wasn't sure whether he was between homes or traversing the farm land. Because the land was level, he decided to enjoy the experience of skiing. After another hundred yards, it suddenly struck Richard that maybe he had gone as far as he should. In the middle of the afternoon there was no one around. Every once in a while a car could be heard on the road that led to his driveway. Sometimes he would hear the engine of a private plane making its approach to the airport about a mile away.

As he thought about what to do next, Richard had a strikingly fearful thought. *I'm on farm land, and I seem to remember that Mindy has often told me about the geese who like to settle in the farm ponds northwest of our house. Have I reached the vicinity of these ponds yet?* He was unable to answer this question and it scared him. *I'd just better get out of here,* he thought. *What if I begin crossing one of these ponds and fall through? Who would be there to hear me? Who would be there to save me?*

At this point, Richard began to breathe more heavily and to tremble.

He had a cell phone in his pocket, but he would feel stupid if he made a 911 call and people came just to take him off a farm field. Being blind was one thing; being blind and pathetic was another.

He stopped and listened for a few minutes. If a car came by, he would know the direction of the road. Once on the road, he was pretty sure that his house was to the south. Eight chances out of ten he would be able to get back to his house if he could get back to the road.

Richard began to dig his poles into the snow after he heard a car's engine several hundred yards off. His hopes rose as his skis glided over the earth. Then, all of a sudden, his skis dipped downward. *Damn! I think I might be on a pond.* He hoped the ice—if that was what he was on—would support him. The crack he next heard sounded like a fatal gunshot, and much to his disbelief, his very strong disbelief, he began sinking in the water. He started to yell, and his yell was taken as an invitation to join in by several hundred crows who were about fifty yards off in several pine trees. Soon the water had reached his waist. It was incredibly cold. At this point he finally thought of his cell phone, but it was too late. His cell phone was in his pants' pocket and was completely wet.

Filled with despair and colder than he thought water could make him, Richard began to cry. *How could such a promising day turn to this?* Just as he was about to give up, he noticed that he was no longer sinking. His skis had apparently hit bottom. *This was better*, he thought, *but it was not perfect. How could he ever get out of this mess?* He turned his head to the left and to the right and sensed no one.

"It is a rather cold day to go water skiing, isn't it honey?" Instantly, he realized Mindy was standing behind him. "Here, wrap this outdoor extension cord around you and I will start to pull. See if you can kick off those damn skis. It's going to be hard enough to get you out of there without them getting caught on the ice. Come on, we've got to do this fast."

The two of them struggled, and soon Richard was back out of the water. "Let's get you out of those wet clothes and into a warm shower," Mindy suggested. "Then we'll go down to the Care Center and let a doctor look at you."

As they waited for the doctor in the Care Center office, Mindy asked Richard why he was out skiing alone. "I just wanted to have a little adventure, honey," he said. She looked at him for about ten seconds and then smiled. "Well," she said, "I guess you did. I guess you did."

CRITTERS

As he looked out the large windows of his three-season room, Charles Jackson scanned his two acres of property with brightening optimism. As had been the case the day before, Charles was not able to see even one woodchuck grazing. He glanced at the large hole under the utility shed, and there was nothing. The two holes approximately twenty yards from the pine trees also showed no sign of habitation. When he turned his attention to the shadowy expanse under his travel trailer, he saw no brown masses chewing on the underside of his recreational vehicle. *I can't believe they are gone*, he thought. *Marsha will be thrilled.*

When Marsha came down to breakfast, Charles excitedly told her of the disappearance of the many woodchucks that had been plaguing him and his property for nearly five years. "I just can't believe it!" he exclaimed. "After all our consternation, these pests are finally gone."

Indeed the woodchucks had occasioned much consternation and the proposal of many plans to remove them. Charles had originally thought of poison. However, Marsha vetoed this plan as the poison might kill other animals in addition to the intended victims, and there was no guarantee that the poison would not be on the grounds when the children came home to visit and brought their dogs. Smoke bombs, loud music, bobcat urine had all been considered and discarded as possible solutions. The same kind of dismissal had been given to "have-a-heart" traps. These devices would trap the woodchuck, but then the woodchuck would have to be transported miles away to another location—usually a state forest. The trouble was that when one woodchuck was eliminated, another usually moved right into the neighborhood, and this is what gave Charles a temporary chill now. He wondered if the woodchucks would come back, but right now they were gone, all gone, and he had done nothing to achieve this happy state of affairs.

"What do you think moved them?" Charles asked.

"I think it was the coyotes," Marsha responded. "I was talking to the people who mow our lawn, and they said that there has been a tremendous influx of coyotes into the area. Nearly everyone has commented on the disappearance of woodchucks on their properties. In fact, they told me they came across a dismembered woodchuck on the Jamison property just the other day."

"Well, that's good news," Charles added. "The coyotes seemed to be performing a critter-cleansing or groundhog genocide. I just wish the coyotes had made this move about five years ago."

Charles and Marsha continued their discussion about the coyotes and what they knew about the presence of these predators on their property. The coyotes, they both agreed, traveled in packs in the neighborhood, and both Charles and Marsha had heard them prowling around the house in the wee hours of the morning. "They seem to pass through fairly quickly in their search for food," Charles commented.

"I occasionally hear them howling when I go to the bathroom in the middle of the night," Marsha said, "but they don't seem to stay in the area very long."

That afternoon, Charles decided to repair his property, and he took a wheelbarrow filled with dirt, a pick ax, and a shovel up into the backyard. As he worked near the utility shed, he smelled a disagreeable odor emanating from the hole, but he wasn't sure if this was the usual smell of a woodchuck's hole or the result of decomposing flesh. Whatever the situation, he was quite happy as he worked and filled in the hole as much as he could with the resources he had available.

As the day progressed, so did Charles' elation. He didn't like critters, any kind of critters. From the smallest insects to mice, rats, snakes, and woodchucks, Charles had nothing but hatred for them all. If he had his way, Noah's Ark would have been torpedoed, and his home and the property around it would be absolutely sterile. Years ago, Marsha had ceased to interject the notion of a pet cat or dog because of Charles' aversion to having any living thing other than human beings complicate his environment. Pets were a responsibility that tied people down, he argued. The other living things all brought dirt and destruction with them. Spiders had their webs, mice had their droppings, and woodchucks could do damage that might easily run into the thousands of dollars.

After a nice dinner where Charles continued to enjoy his unexpected turn of luck, he told Marsha that he was going to extend his celebration by going out to one of his favorite bars and singing karaoke. He told Marsha that he anticipated that the celebration would be such that he would really like a ride from her to his favorite lounge, and later he would take a cab ride home.

It was quite a night for Charles at the bar. Everyone sensed his extremely upbeat persona during the evening. His karaoke selections reflected the joy he felt, and he laughed and smiled throughout his performances. He toasted coyotes several times, and he probably drank more than he should have, maybe much more than he should have. He stayed until last call, and then took a cab home. By the time the cab left him off on his country driveway, he was having a bit of difficulty forming his words. The driver asked him if he needed some assistance getting into his house, but Charles waved him off, and the cab disappeared into the darkness of the countryside.

Charles watched the lights of the cab disappear and then tried to find his keys to the door. He had several keys on his chain, and he was upset that Marsha neglected to put on the outside lights. As he tried to identify the proper key to the outside door, he felt a strange sensation, and the driveway began to spin and tilt. He felt he was losing his balance and sank down to one knee. Soon a wave of turbulence overcame him, and he laid his entire body on the asphalt and lost consciousness. How long he stayed in that state he did not know, but something had brought him back to consciousness. Something was brushing across his face, and he sensed the presence of numerous creatures around him. As he opened his eyes, he couldn't identify the shapes around him in the darkness. Then, suddenly, the half-moon broke out from behind a cloud, and he saw that he was the midst of a pack of animals. At first he wondered if a bunch of woodchucks had come by for accommodations. Then he saw with horror the sparkling of the moonlight on the teeth and in the eyes of many hungry coyotes.

BIRD ISLAND

Sipping his coffee, Jack LaGrange looked over the side of his tour boat at the almost glassy sea that would be his path out of this small harbor of Cape Breton Island. The light fog had begun to lift, and the sun, like a low-wattage bulb, was attempting to make its presence known over this calm sea. Jack was the captain and chief guide on the *Cormorant II*, a tour boat he had piloted for almost thirty years now. He grunted as he looked at his ceramic coffee mug where several letters had worn off the marketing decal that was affixed to the outside of the mug. Instead of Bird Island Tours, Jack had only " ird Island rs." Yet, he thought to himself, that is what is ours—ird Island.

Swallowing his last gulp, he looked toward the land to see if he could identify Meg, his college-age assistant, who would be leading a group of perhaps twenty tourists down to the boat any minute now. He recalled when he had been a college student and had started working for Bird Island Tours. He had been a better than average student in natural sciences at Cape Breton College, but he hadn't exactly been sure what he wanted to do with his potential degree. Then, after his junior year, he got this job working on the boat. For a college kid, the money was good. At the end of the summer, he found out he could have a position as the off-season man at the adjacent campground. It was something concrete, and he needed a break. So, much to his uncle and aunt's dismay, he took an official leave from Cape Breton College, a leave that was now twenty-nine years longer than he ever expected it to be.

At first, being a student helper was a lot of fun. Wasn't it always part of every college student's mantra to have experiences to "meet new people"? Then when meeting new people didn't seem to stand the test of time, the previous captain, Ray Reynolds, decided to retire. After just three years, Jack found himself the captain.

In the beginning, Jack liked the theatricality and attention of it all.

He liked explaining to the crowds the various species that inhabited Bird Island. In addition to discussing the birds, he could often point out the sea creatures that sometimes made themselves visible. Seals, turtles, migrating whales, and an occasional shark would provide him with opportunities to display his expertise, much to the wonder of the generally ignorant crowd that boarded the tour boat. But that was twenty-seven years ago, much like the letters on the coffee cup, and the experience of being the naturalist guide had lost more than a little something.

Finally, he saw Meg rounding the corner with the fairly large group of tourists. His heart sank as he saw a couple of strollers mixed in with the crowd. Crying and screaming toddlers weren't much of a problem on a breezy day, but the quiet of this morning would surely enhance the screeches that he knew would come about twenty minutes into the voyage.

With much effort, Jack forced the muscles of his mouth to form a smile as the tourists approached the gangway, but the twinkle in his eye was no longer available. That light had been extinguished over a decade ago.

"Welcome to the *Cormorant II*, folks," Jack intoned. "Please watch your step as you board the vessel."

"That's the entire group, Captain," Meg yelled.

"In that case, Meg, man the ropes as we get ready to depart," Jack barked back.

As the boat pulled away from the dock, Jack once again welcomed the passengers and enthusiastically listed all the marine animals and birds that the *Cormorant II* might run into this day. His excitement had a positive effect on his passengers, but both he and Meg gave credit to his theatricality for this enthusiasm rather than any continuing love that he still had for his work.

However, on the way out to Bird Island, an event occurred that did get Jack's heart beating a bit quicker. Off to starboard, an eight-foot blue shark suddenly surfaced. Knowing the frenzy of crowds whenever any sort of marine apparition occurs, Jack spoke calmly into the microphone, "Folks, if you would like to see a shark, there is one about twenty feet to the right of the boat." Predictably, the crowd moved in an almost hysterical way to the starboard rail. Cameras and pointing fingers were everywhere. While the boat listed a bit to the right, Jack was, as always, pleased with the kind of vessel he captained. He had heard of other vessels where a passenger stampede had almost capsized the boat. The *Cormorant II* was much more stable than that. Although it certainly could not be called a fast or sleek boat, it was indeed a very stable boat.

With the thrill of something memorable under everyone's belt, Jack knew this would be a relatively happy cruise, even though one of the toddlers had begun the predictable wailing of unhappiness that always seemed part of a toddler's experience when placed within a confined space.

In twenty minutes, the boat reached the climax of the tour as Jack slowed the motor to provide an appreciation of Bird Island. It was a rocky outcropping of perhaps two football fields long with a pile of rocks in its middle that ascended almost one hundred feet high. There were a few bushes and hundreds of birds of all sorts. Cormorants, gulls, terns, and, of course, the highly-prized puffin were all part of this avian community. What fed this community, and what perhaps drew the wayward shark, was the high quantity of fish that was available in the waters that surrounded the island. Since this was a protected natural area, there had generally been stability in the bird population over the decades. Jack made this point loud and clear to the passengers who were delighting in the variety of the island.

"However," Jack said, "this stability has changed recently. I am going to show you what the cause for this change has been." At this point he started the motors again and began to circle the island. "Somehow or other over the past year a previously unknown predator has entered the island eco-system. I'm hoping we can see him. We can usually find him if we look hard enough. Ah, there he is! Look to the left of that great boulder."

As the passengers looked, most of them could hardly believe their eyes. There on Bird Island, a sanctuary for birds that had existed for hundreds, perhaps thousands, of years, was a lone bobcat. It was obviously doing very well. His coat was sleek; his body seemed firm and muscular. The passengers could see him poking his nose into crevices and looking in all directions, searching for prey.

"Naturalists haven't figured out how this bobcat got out here," Jack announced. "Some have postulated that he came out on an ice floe over the winter. We get ice around the island and also around the main island just about every year. The bobcat could have gotten caught on an ice floe that broke off and came out here. That's one theory. The other is that somehow he got on a piece of debris that floated to the island. In any event, over the last year, he's killed about a third of the population."

"Can't he be killed or captured?" said one of the passengers.

"No," Jack responded; "the regulations that govern this natural environment insist that there will be no human intervention in the natural processes of this ecology."

"Can the bobcat eat the entire bird population?" inquired another passenger.

"No," said Meg. "According to those scientists who studied the island, the bird population has probably stabilized now. The bobcat has eaten all he needs and the birds continue to procreate in such a way that the population has stabilized."

"In any case," said Jack, "what you have seen today, folks, is the battle between prey and predator. You saw it here on Bird Island with the bobcat and the birds, and you got a sense of it in watching that big shark glide around looking for fish to eat in the waters off the island."

When the boat finally got to shore and the passengers disembarked, Meg said to Jack, "Well, another in the books, huh, Jack?"

"Yeah, Meg, until our evening cruise at 5:30."

Jack and Meg did indeed do another cruise that evening, and for Jack it was like the myth of Sisyphus. Another cruise was another rolling of the boulder up the mountain only to have it come down one more time. Jack wondered how many more times he could endure the process, how many more times he could smile falsely about the same animals with the same forced enthusiasm. He had also begun to wonder how much time was left for him to do something else, and what that something else could be. He really had never tried to do anything else but this, and he had not thought about his future, only about the grueling present. As a result, he had set aside little money for retirement, something that wasn't very unusual for people in his position. These thoughts about changing had been on his mind for several years now, but he just never seemed to be able to take the initiative to leave this job and go on to something else. He knew that something would have to force him to go, something that would carry some inevitability with it.

As they walked away from *Cormorant II* that evening, Meg asked Jack if he wanted to grab some pizza and some beer. Jack responded that he appreciated the offer but he had another commitment that evening.

"Okay, Jack, I'll see you tomorrow."

As Jack drove through the darkness, he felt an excitement that he had not felt for a while. It was exhilarating doing something for himself for a change and not worrying about how the passengers felt and whether or not they were going to be satisfied with their cruise. Now it was his turn to do something about his own experience.

Although he had only been to this cabin once before, he seemed to remember the way. There was a long dirt road and then a house with just a small light burning inside. When he pulled up in the driveway, a man immediately came out of the house and led Jack to the barn. The man showed Jack a large rectangular structure covered by a tarp. Jack glanced under the tarp, nodded, and handed the man $750 in cash. They loaded the object on Jack's truck, and he swiftly drove back to the dock and the *Cormorant II*.

Using a couple of wooded planks, he dragged his cargo onto the boat. It was nearly midnight, and there wasn't a soul around. Jack took the boat out to Bird Island and got as close as he could to its rocky shore. To meet safety requirements, the *Cormorant II* was equipped with a wonderful depth finder, and Jack kept his eyes glued to the screen until he was only about seven or eight yards from the shore. At this point, Jack lugged his heavy cargo onto the rail, tilted it towards the water and tripped a release that sent the contents of the rectangular box splashing into the sea. There was thrashing, some gurgling, and then the sure sound of padded feet scratching on the stony beach. Then crying and screeching sounds began to develop. *Ah*, thought Jack to himself, *she's finally worked the gag off that we had in her mouth.* At this point a caterwaul was heard for the first time, a cry that was soon answered by another caterwaul from another part of the island. *Now that there are two of you*, Jack thought, *maybe we can clear out the rest of the birds from this damn island. Certainly if you can't do it by yourselves, you will be able to do it with your children.* "Well, so long lovers," Jack muttered as he reversed the *Cormorant II* and set his course back to the dock.

About two years later, Jack received word that the owners of Bird Island Tours were closing down operations. The bobcats on the island had destroyed the bird population, and although the bobcats' kittens had been of interest to some of the tourists, their developing starvation after the demise of their food supply was not a pleasant thing to see for most of the guests who rode the *Cormorant II*.

Jack was surprised at the amount of his severance package, but even more surprised by an offer that was made to him to captain another tour boat on another part of Cape Breton Island. He wanted no more of boats and tourists and phony enthusiasm. When Meg asked him how he thought the second bobcat got on the island, he responded by saying, "Some kind of debris, I guess. You know, there are lots of things in this world that just seem to happen; nobody knows why. That's probably what's happened here."

DRAGS AND DUNGEONS

Susan Malley grimaced as she left the hotel and headed for the tour bus thirty yards away. She was disappointed that this eighth day of her trip to Ireland was going to be another day of drizzle and temperatures in the fifties. She and her husband were, generally, enjoying the trip, but a nice day or two wouldn't hurt. In Dublin, the attractions and places of interest had been many, and the urban environment could dazzle anyone even during showers. Galway, too, with its pubs, Irish dancing, and numerous shops wasn't dependent upon nature and her blessing for happiness. Now, however, as Susan and her husband Peter traveled the countryside, some sun on the Emerald Isle would be most welcomed.

As she approached the bus, she began to hear the other problem with this AAA tour of Ireland and Scotland. It was a large man almost six-foot four-inches tall who had a disagreeable ability to draw attention to himself and to disrupt the rather intelligent comments of the tour's knowledgeable guide. The guide, Erin O'Leary, was a true personification of the Irish ideal. Her dancing eyes, frequent smiles, and lyrical voice had charmed nearly everyone on the tour. Her knowledge of Irish history and culture had made such an impression that the members of the tour were always ready when she grabbed hold of the microphone in the bus. Only Gerald Weatherby caused problems. For some reason that only a psychiatrist might be able to fathom, he was not charmed by Miss O'Leary; furthermore, he seemed to make it a point every day that he, and not Ireland or Miss O'Leary, should be the focus of the tour's attention.

And so, Susan sighed when she heard Gerald's voice. She thought of it as an annoying voice, even though when anyone might first hear it, his voice would seem little different from the average. Initially the other members of the tour had complained to each other. Then they complained to Miss O'Leary. Some heard her very gently chastise Gerald for his constant talking and his interruptions of her lectures. He told her he was sorry, but he had to be himself. As a paying customer, he had every right, he told her, to express himself when and where he wanted. Furthermore, if anyone happened to be displeased with him, that person should talk to him and not to the guide of the group.

When word got around that Gerald wanted to be talked to, the members of the tour obliged him. Indeed, everyone had something to say to him. Some of the women talked to him gently and patiently about his lack of manners. Some of the men yelled at him. In fact, Peter and a tourist named Ivan from the Ukraine almost came to blows with Gerald. However, the outcomes of all these exchanges were the same—Gerald kept doing what he was doing.

Now, half way through the tour, the group was at a decision point. They were either going to accept Gerald's behavior, or they were going to have to do something about it. They had already made him a pariah and exiled him to the back of the bus. No one would initiate a conversation with him, and no one would talk to him at meals. Yet, all of this made no difference to Gerald, and his behavior always remained just one slight degree below the level of transgression that would get him expelled from the group.

Despite the rainy weather and Gerald Weatherby, Susan was looking forward to this particular day. The tour's destination was Bunratty Castle and the cultural village that surrounded it. Susan knew that the castle was in good shape, and friends of hers had told her that their visit there had been one of the highlights of their trip.

As the bus rolled along, Erin pointed out both the geological and the cultural features of the Irish landscape. With about fifteen minutes to go, Erin began to describe the castle and its history. She pointed out that some of the features of the castle, such as its winding staircases, were designed to be quite useful to castle inhabitants in case of an attack. Right-handed attackers would be cramped against a wall and not able to wield their weapons effectively when they were coming up the stairs. The right-handed defenders, however, who would be coming down the stairs, had no wall to impair their right-handed sword play and held a tremendous advantage.

Another structural element of the castle was the line of demarcation in the large hall that served to house the castle's garrison. This line divided the soldiers from their officers. On the officers' side, there was a large fireplace—the only source of warmth for this part of the castle. The rank-and-file soldiers were in the distant half on the far side of the room where it was much cooler and damp during many months of the year. It was difficult to miss the social distinction that was made obvious by the line of demarcation.

Among many other fascinating tidbits about the castle was the dungeon. Susan was quite interested in the fact that men were literally thrown into the dungeon, and that once in this pit, nine or ten feet below any path to escape, prospects for a long and rewarding life were slim indeed.

When the bus finally arrived at the castle, it was about forty-five minutes from closing time. Traffic on the small highway and some delays during lunch at one of the previous stops had put a bit of pressure on the day's agenda. Yet now they were here, and it was time to gobble up as much culture as time would allow. Horribly, as Erin began her presentation about the castle, Gerald decided it was his time to gain attention, and he began spouting off about all the reasons why he liked castles, what he thought about castles he had seen before and how they compared to Bunratty, and what he would do if he were creating a tour of this very site. Several of the men asked him to shut up, but as usual he was oblivious. Erin tried to continue as best as she could, but Gerald's babbling and the angry responses of the other tour members blotted out much of what she had to say.

"Peter, we've got to stop this," Susan said. "We each paid $3,500 for this trip, and we still have a week to go in Scotland. It's not that Gerald is a jerk; he's a thieving jerk. He's robbing us of the fun, knowledge and pleasure we certainly have paid for." Peter could see the seriousness in his wife's eyes and hear it in her voice. He wanted to put a stop to Gerald, too, but he was unsure what to do.

As a final part of the castle tour, the group descended to the dungeon. It was a tight fit to get everyone down there, and it was quite dark. As usual, Gerald wanted to be in a place of prominence, so he got right to the edge of the pit as Erin began her talk. Again, Gerald interrupted much of what Erin spoke, and she eventually gave up by telling the group they could spend a few more minutes in the dungeon, but that she was going out to talk to the driver and to get the bus warmed up. She would expect the group in about five minutes.

When Erin left, Peter walked over to Gerald and began to ask him a few questions. Susan was a bit startled that her husband would actually be talking to Gerald. Peter asked Gerald about what Gerald thought was the worst dungeon he had ever seen. Then he asked him about how long he thought anyone could live in a dungeon, and whether Gerald believed there were any dungeons in use in Europe. Gerald seemed delighted to have become the new guide on site and exploded dramatically about all his opinions. Finally, Peter asked Gerald if he could explain the significance of some of the molding on the far wall of the dungeon. As Gerald turned to examine this molding, Peter pushed him from behind with all of his might. Gerald fell over into the dungeon, hitting his head on the stones and jagged rocks on the floor. The group moved to the edge of the platform and looked down. They saw plenty of blood but little movement. Silently, they got on the bus. When Erin asked if everyone was on the bus, the group said that they were except for Gerald.

"What happened to him?" Erin asked.

"He said there were a few more things he wanted to see in the castle. We told him he only had a few minutes, but he said he would hurry."

"Yeah," said Peter. "The last time I saw him was when I was leaving the dungeon. I turned around and I saw him leaning over trying to get a good look at some artistically crafted molding that was on the side of the dungeon wall." No one on the bus had any other memories of what Gerald was doing when they last saw him.

When the police came, their memories did not change. Gerald had been on the edge of the platform above the dungeon and had been talking to Peter about some moulding. The police seemed satisfied with this explanation of the accident and permitted the tour to go on its way.

As the bus began its quiet advance down the highway, all agreed that Bunratty Castle had been all they had wanted it to be and more, and they all looked forward to the next week of their tour.

COMPETITION

Rob winced as he looked at the painted marking on the asphalt highway. He saw the number 16 clearly displayed. He knew that in just a little over ten miles he would be finishing his first marathon. He would be finishing, that is, if the pain in his left knee, which started a minute ago, would subside. In all his previous running, he had never encountered a pain like this—sharp, insistent, and suggestive of something really wrong. He was upset that he was having this pain because he had approached this marathon with the clear idea that he was not going to "hit the wall." He had been training for several years, and he was running 40 to 48 miles per week in anticipation of this big event. Even today, he was very careful in his planning. Over the first sixteen miles, he was running about 8.5 minutes for each mile—not a break-neck pace, but one which had promised a comfortable and satisfying run.

Now, all of these plans seemed to have been made in vain. Feeling like a charter member of the "walk-it-off" club, Rob continued to jog and to gauge the increase or decrease of pain that he felt. The gods, however, were going to be good today. As he ran his next half mile, Rob began to feel the pain lessen. After another mile, the pain was entirely gone. Rob could hardly believe it.

Yet, even as he began to feel safe and smugly satisfied, he noticed that the weather was beginning to change. A very dark nimbus cloud descended upon the race course, and temperatures which had been pushing sixty degrees started to fall quite rapidly. Within a few minutes, the wind had picked up to twenty mph; the temperature had dropped into the high forties, and it started to hail. Because it had been so nice at the beginning of the race, Rob had no protection on his arms except for his T-shirt. His legs, numb to the cold after months of training in all weather conditions above freezing, were stung by little bits of hail but were not particularly uncomfortable. His upper body was another issue. Rob felt cold and chilled and hoped that the nasty weather would soon pass.

Miraculously enough, the gods spared Rob again. The dark cloud passed; the winds calmed, and temperatures began to move higher. At the 19 mile mark, Rob resumed a comfortable and sustainable pace. For the next five miles, he moved along easily and began to pass other runners. It wasn't that Rob was fast; it was that the other runners had slowed down. Some had slowed down quite a bit. In his conversations with other runners before the race, Rob had learned that some of them trained as little as fifteen miles per week. In addition, many of these runners had been filled with race euphoria and had set off on a pace that certainly would had been admirable if the runners could maintain it, but was very dangerous if the runners could not. These runners were "hitting the wall." It was a risk that a runner would take if he wanted to get every last ounce of energy out of his body. Rob had decided that he did not want to do this, so now he loped along, not risking and not pushing.

With a little over two miles to go, the race reached a very discouraging point. Much to the disbelief of many of the runners, the highway began to climb a long and steep farm hill. All of a sudden, runners began to stop running. They walked along the shoulder of the road, obviously beaten by the topography and totally spent physically. A girl in her early twenties who had passed Rob a long time ago now appeared in front of him. She was slender and attractive and wearing a very cute pair of striped running shorts. She had not started to walk yet, but her running form had totally degenerated. She no longer proceeded in a straight line and moved as if she were in some sort of drunken delirium. She stumbled toward the shoulder and then slapped her running shoes in the other direction until she was wobbling on the yellow center line of the highway. She was doing a jogger's slalom, and Rob seriously wondered if she were going to collapse. After making one last pass toward the center yellow lines, she veered back to the shoulder and came to a complete stop.

As Rob passed the girl in the striped shorts, he could see no one immediately ahead. He was still jogging, and he was about half way up the steep hill. He was tired and wished that he were at the end of the race, but he was determined not to stop going up the hill. He thought about pushing himself to gain a bit more speed but decided against it.

As he reached the top of the hill, Rob spied the final distance marker. It happily proclaimed that Rob had reached the twenty-five mile point. He knew that only 1.2 miles separated him from the finish line. As he savored this information, Rob noticed another runner about one hundred yards from him. As the road surface was becoming slightly downhill, Rob picked up his pace. He got within fifty yards of the other male runner, and still there was no sign the other runner was going to respond to a challenge from the rear. As the incline of the descent grew, Rob quickened his pace. At about twenty-five yards from the man, Rob saw his competitor glance around and see him. The other runner immediately picked up his pace, and Rob knew he was in for a fight.

Rob answered his opponent's increase in speed with an increase of his own. Rob was delighted to see how much he had in reserve, and as he put the pressure on, he began to gain on the man, foot by foot, every ten steps or so even though it was obvious that the other runner was running as hard as he could. At a final turn in the highway, Rob could see the steel bridge that marked the end of the race. There were three hundred yards to go, and Rob was sprinting. As he passed the other runner, Rob saw him glance his way for just a second. He also noticed that the man was grimacing in pain and giving the race everything he had, yet it was not enough. By the time Rob crossed the bridge, he was a full forty yards ahead of his competitor. Crossing the finish line, he heard his time—3 hours 42 minutes and 55 seconds.

As he began his cool-down walk, Rob searched the crowd for his wife. Quickly she appeared beside him, holding a can of beer for Rob to enjoy. Rob hugged her and drank the beer. He noticed that his breathing was already just about normal. Amber, his wife, asked him if he felt exhausted. Rob responded that he felt just fine. In fact, he thought he could probably run at least two or three more miles. They both chuckled, and Rob sat down on a bench next to Amber.

As he sat down, Rob noticed that the man that he had beaten in the last mile was talking nearby to several friends. He excitedly told his friends that his total time for the race was 3 hours 43 minutes and 6 seconds. He said that he couldn't believe that he almost kept up with this guy who came flying by him. After all, the most he had trained for the event was twenty miles per week. "The best part of the whole thing," he said, "was that I have no regrets that I could have done better. I ran as hard as I could for as long as I could. I can hardly stand up now; I don't have any energy left."

Hearing these words, Rob felt a heaviness come over him. The elation he had felt upon crossing the bridge left him. Standing up briskly and grabbing his wife's arm, he walked quickly to his car parked several blocks away. Sitting in the passenger seat, he took off his running shoes. He saw the slogan on the back of the shoe, "Go for it," and he looked at his feet and a tear fell from his eye.

MORAL FAILURES

Howard Jensen sat quietly in his SUV in the darkness and looked down from the hill where he was parked to Scott's Trailer Estates. Of particular interest to him was the trailer on Lot 17. This was the home of Jimmy Tripp, and, although it was a few minutes after midnight, Howard knew there was no one home because he had been watching the trailer for several hours. This was his second night of observing Tripp's trailer. Last night he had sat until dawn waiting for Jimmy Tripp to come back home, but as the sun began to lighten the skies, there was still no sign of Mr. Tripp, so Howard had gone home to bed.

As he waited for Tripp to arrive, Howard thought about all the things, the very terrible things, that had happened over the last several years. It all started with the death of his daughter Lizzy. She was a wonderful child, an only child, and the center of Howard's existence. Lizzy was bright and service oriented. She had studied hard at school and had achieved the professional distinction of becoming a Physician's Assistant. She worked in a pair of clinics for the poor located in the heart of the city. She usually worked more than sixty hours a week, but she loved what she was doing, and she loved the impact she had on her patients. Their lives were much better because of the service she was able to provide. However, this all ended on a tragic night four years ago when her small sedan was hit by a pickup truck driven by Jimmy Tripp.

The police quickly determined that the collision was entirely Tripp's fault. He was incredibly intoxicated, and the alcohol content in his blood was nearly three times the legal limit. Furthermore, this was not Jimmy's first recorded incident of DWI. He had been arrested and convicted for driving while intoxicated twice before; however, in those previous instances, no one had died. This time someone had died, killed instantly by a man who had never contributed to the welfare of a single human being.

Howard's thoughts then turned to the pain of the trial and even more so to the great frustration of the sentencing hearing. Tripp was charged with vehicular manslaughter. Howard remembered how difficult it was to sit through the trial, especially when the defense lawyer tried to picture Tripp as anything but the dirt-bag everyone knew he was. Excuses, explanations, and sugar-coating were all the stuff of the defense's attempt to lessen the responsibility that surely was Jimmy Tripp's. The one thing that clearly was left out of the presentations of the defense attorney was the truth. Fortunately, the jury knew exactly what had happened and returned a guilty verdict in less than an hour.

Yet, the verdict brought little satisfaction. At the sentencing hearing, Lizzy's family members had the opportunity to make statements to the court. In one way or another, they all talked about the beautiful human being that had been lost to them, lost forever. There were tears and anguish. When the family members were finished, members of the medical community and a few of Lizzy's patients came forward to share their loss and their sense of outrage about what had happened. Then Jimmy had a chance to speak. His lawyer had told him that contrition, regret, and an apology were important if Jimmy wanted to get any reduction in his sentence. If his comments were believable to the judge, the defense lawyer argued, Jimmy might save himself a number of months in prison. No one in the family cared a bit whether Jimmy regretted what he did or not; the fact was he had killed Lizzy. That was all that mattered, and Jimmy could do nothing to change that. For the family, all Jimmy could do was pay the legal maximum for what he had done.

Howard was prepared for the sentence that was to be delivered. He had talked to the prosecutors and knew that legally the judge could do just so much. When a sentence of three years with the possibility of parole for good behavior was handed down, many in the courtroom gasped. How could this be? A life was tragically ended—a life that that under average circumstances would have continued for another fifty years. This productive life had been cut short by a thoughtless and criminal act. How could fifty years of Lizzy's life be equated with only three of Jimmy Tripp's life?

Howard had seen other victims of crime experience similar injustices. In news reports, he had often seen these people in the deepest pain break down emotionally after the sentencing had been rendered.

Yet, he never heard them follow up on their outrage. As he thought about it, he concluded that this reaction was a moral lapse on the part of the family and friends of the victim. If an injustice had been done, it should be righted. However, he never heard of anything actually happening to the perpetrator. As far as Howard knew, perpetrators went to prison, didn't rock the boat, were released early, and went on their way. Occasionally, he would hear of a released criminal who eventually committed additional crimes and got back into the judicial system. Most of the time, however, he never heard of them again.

For Howard, this moral failure, this lack of moral courage to stand up for what was right, was parallel to what happened in the area of abortion. Howard knew lots of people who felt the way he did and opposed abortion and considered it to be murder. *If abortion is the murder of babies*, Howard thought, *how can we stand by and let it happen? If abortion is the killing of babies, is the carrying of protest signs and the selling of flowers the best we can do? We should all be ashamed of ourselves,* Howard speculated, *for lacking the courage to do anything about that.* In the case of his own daughter Lizzy, Howard was ready to cross the line.

And so Howard sat in the darkness. He had planned his imposition of justice in a way that would allow him a chance to escape. He would not be crushed if the authorities caught him, but settling the score would be more satisfying if he didn't have to go through the penalties that the law rather than justice would heap upon him. A good part of his plan had come from his knowledge of what the snipers had done around Washington, D.C. a few years earlier. By using long shot rifles, these killers had been able to attack people in the Washington area with impunity for several weeks.

Now, Howard had placed himself on a hill about a half mile from Jimmy Tripp's trailer. Howard was a great shot and had a good weapon. The place where he sat in his SUV was secluded, and he was able to drive his vehicle off the road far enough so that he would not be seen by passers-by. If he were seen, it would appear to be just a parked vehicle. In addition, all of the windows that faced the road were heavily tinted. The only window that was not tinted was the windshield, and this was the window that was giving Howard a view of Tripp's trailer.

At approximately 2:45 a.m. Howard saw some lights coming up to Tripp's trailer. As a man got out of the driver's seat, the light in the trailer park was good enough for Howard to see that it was the killer of his Lizzy. Howard took his rifle, an unregistered weapon he had received when his grandfather had died over twenty years ago, and began to sight it on Jimmy. As Jimmy went to unlock his trailer door, Howard whispered, "This is for you, Lizzy." He pulled the trigger twice and watched Tripp fall to the ground. The shots had made noise, but the silence that followed had quickly re-enveloped the night. Howard started his SUV and followed the escape route he had planned. He had one more stop to make. When he got near the bridge by a small but deep silty lake about two miles from his home, Howard wiped off the rifle to remove any and all prints. The ammunition chamber was empty, and when he tossed the gun into the lake, he knew it would be buried under silt. When he arrived home, he watched a recording of that night's late night comedy shows. After viewing the shows, he laundered his clothes in the washing machine and took a long shower. Then he went to bed.

As he expected, the police stopped by his house the next day to ask some questions. They asked him if he had any guns. Howard pointed to his rifle collection in the recreation room. When the police asked if they could look at the rifles, he was quite obliging. Howard knew that no evidence would be found there. When he was asked where he had been the previous night, Howard indicated that he had had a couple of beers and watched some television. He even threw in a humorous comment that had been made on one of the shows. When the police left, Howard went into his living room and looked at a picture of Lizzy that had been taken the Christmas before she had died. A few tears welled up in his eyes as he kissed Lizzy's picture. "Rest easy, my dear, rest easy."

PITCHING ON THE BLACK

Dave opened his right eye as a narrow ray of sun began to heat his face. Suddenly conscious of the humid air he was breathing, he grunted his disapproval. It was going to be another terribly hot and humid July day in Bayonne, New Jersey, a small city located on New York Harbor. Such miserably oppressive days were common enough in Bayonne in the summer time, but their commonness did not lessen their unpleasantness. Once the temperature got over ninety degrees and the humidity approached 70 percent, the air hung on everyone like a heavy wet blanket that made movements sluggish and produced prodigious amounts of perspiration as soon as one stepped in the smothering embrace of the stifling air. As Dave considered the weather he was about to face, he felt a twinge of disappointment. He and his brother Chuck had planned a full day of baseball for this Thursday at Hudson County Park. It wasn't going to be a large team game; it was just going to be a game between the two brothers. All of their friends had gone with their families down to the Shore.

While Dave and Chuck were not fortunate enough to go to the beach this particularly hot day, they were lucky enough to have each other. Dave was fourteen, and his brother Chuck was thirteen. Chuck was born eleven months after Dave, and their closeness in age gave each one a built-in friend and playmate. At this point in their lives, Dave was a half-a-head taller than Chuck and outweighed him by fifteen pounds. Chuck, however, was a bit more athletic and coordinated, and so the physical differences on the playing field just about evened out.

As Dave was rolling off the top bunk and heading for the floor, he poked his right foot into Chuck's side. "Get up! Get up! You are not going to be able to avoid a thrashing by lying in bed all day," Dave jeered.

"Yeah, yeah," Chuck responded as he opened both of his eyes, "in your dreams, in your dreams."

An hour later, Dave and Chuck were completing their half mile walk to the park. They both enjoyed the fact that they had invented a way of playing baseball with only one player on each side. The first requirement was to find a backstop where one could throw a pitched ball and be able to retrieve it quickly. There were three large baseball diamonds in the park, and each was equipped with backstops that extended up along the first and the third base lines. These diamonds were usually deserted during the day, and they certainly were deserted on an oppressively hot day like this. Since late-day thunderstorms were common during the summer, the dirt infields of the diamonds were usually marked by a few puddles and some areas of mud. As a result, it made little sense to try to pitch from the dirt infield to the backstop behind home plate. Similarly, the first base backstop area was unattractive. Both Dave and Chuck were right-handed batters. If they pitched to the first-base fencing, the batter would inevitability pull many pitches onto the wet and muddy infield. This was not desirable. Therefore, Dave and Chuck almost always played their games along the third-base line where the batted balls would dependably wind up on the grassy outfield surface.

Even more important for the success of their game was the emphasis that Chuck and Dave put on their imaginations and good faith. They usually brought a piece of cardboard to serve as home plate, but with no umpire to call balls and strikes, quick agreement on close pitches was critically important. When the batter hit a ball, both agreement and imagination came into play. Where they were playing, there were no foul lines, no infield, no bases, and no other players. Both Chuck and Dave had a virtual idea of where the foul lines would be and where the other players would be stationed if they existed. With their imaginary field and players in place, Chuck and Dave found easy agreement on ground balls. They were almost always outs. Pop-ups too were easy to rule on as clear outs. Short and medium fly balls to the outfield also were considered outs. Short and long line drives were considered singles and doubles. The occasional long drive usually gained recognition as a triple or home run. To anyone who might have watched their games— although no one ever did—it was clear that, in the imaginary world of these brothers, Willie Mays was not playing in the outfield. No long drives were ever caught by a Hall of Fame fielder.

If the rules and the personnel were simple, the equipment was even more so. There was no batting helmet. There were no spiked baseball shoes. There was only one bat—a black Eddie Stanky bat that both boys loved. It seemed to be the right weight and length for both of them, and they both cherished the large "sweet spot"—a spot that allowed each of them to drive a ball from time to time an impressive distance. They agreed that driving a baseball a long distance was one of the great feelings in life, like hooking a large, spirited fish or hitting a diving board right in that place where the diver's spring would be the greatest.

The most critical items of all were the baseballs. Dave and Chuck were not from a rich family, yet they needed many baseballs. Without a good supply of balls, the game would really slow down as the pitcher would have to run out into the outfield again and again to retrieve batted balls.

To meet this need for the many balls required, Dave and Chuck would bring anything that would resemble a baseball to the field. One or two of the balls were just slightly scuffed, and one of these might even be included in an organized game. Another two of the balls had developed some split stitching. With these balls, the cover of the baseball might be slightly curled on a very small section of the ball's surface. On the plus side, these balls would often produce some interesting curving or knuckleball action when the pitcher threw them in just the right way.

Another cheap import ball from Asia was also part of the inventory. This ball was so poorly made that upon several uses, part of the ball surface would be flattened. This resulted from the fact that the interior of the ball was not wound yarn but merely paper. When one of these balls eventually disintegrated, the boys would have fun pulling out the paper and looking at the Chinese or Japanese writing—the boys couldn't figure out which—that often was printed on the paper. The Asian ball was about 30 percent lighter than the regulation baseball. Because it was so much lighter, the ball floated a bit more. It was harder for the pitcher to achieve the same velocity with the Asian ball as he did with the other balls. However, although it was usually easier to hit, the Asian ball did not travel as far as the other balls, and so the advantage the batter had in hitting the ball was offset by the limited distance he could drive it.

While the Asian ball was lighter than normal, the last ball in the collection was heavier. When a ball had finally lost its cover, Dave and Chuck would sometimes provide themselves with another ball by covering the yarn of the coverless ball with black electrician's tape. It took a great deal of tape to cover the ball in such a way that it could be used again and again, and this tape added a significant amount of weight to the ball, as the tape was much heavier than the cow hide and stitching that it was replacing. The taped ball was heavy, noticeably heavy. It always seemed to Dave that the weight of this ball enabled the pitcher to throw it a little bit faster than any of the other balls in the collection. It also seemed to Dave as a batter that when Chuck threw the taped ball to the plate, it was harder to see. In addition, the ball did not seem to spring off the bat the way the slightly scuffed balls did. While the tape used on the ball might be an electrician's friend, Dave always considered the taped ball to be an ally of the pitcher.

Anyone who looked over the selection of the six balls available to the boys would see that there could be some strategy developed about which balls could be used in which situation. The boys themselves were students of the game, and they saw some rules would have to be made about which balls would be played and in which order. Because they wanted their game to be as close to regulation and reality as it could be, the boys agreed that the scuffed balls—the best of the lot—would always be used first. Because the chain-length fencing of the back stop would usually drop the balls at the batter's feet, these balls could be thrown back to the pitcher and used again and again until they had been batted out into the field beyond the pitcher. After these balls were no longer available, the two balls of split stitches would be used. If strikeouts or come-backers to the pitcher occurred in a particular half inning, these four balls might be the only ones used, and the boys would not have to resort to the lowest level of baseball. However, when it was necessary to use the Asian ball or the taped ball, the boys agreed that either ball could be used first. They also thought that choosing a particular ball represented a kind of strategy. A change-up, for example, would probably work better with the Asian ball. The taped ball, on the other hand, would help the pitcher throw a very challenging fast ball.

Neither boy was looking forward to retrieving baseballs on this day. Despite being on the ball field for only a few minutes, a dark ring of forehead sweat was already visible on the cloth of their baseball caps. It was only late morning, but the temperature was already in the high 80s. The humidity, clearly observable in the hazy sunshine, had begun to cause somewhat labored breathing as well as an overall feeling of physical discomfort. It was a very hot day. The only other human activity in this fairly large park was five hundred yards away from the boys where a lone lawnmower did its work on the expansive grass fields.

Once they had gotten in their usual field and arranged their equipment, Chunk and Dave flipped a coin to see who would bat first. Dave won the toss and decided to be the home team, and, therefore batted second. As Chuck went over to home plate—the cardboard home plate that they both chuckled about—Dave asked Chuck if he could take a couple of pitches so that he could warm up appropriately. As both boys loosened up, each felt confidence surging within himself. Chuck had been playing ball as long as Dave. He had started when he was eight; Dave had started when he was nine. Chuck had always shown athletic ability. In fact, in the last year he had actually started several games as a pitcher during his final season for his Little League team, so he felt that he was about as far along as a young boy could be at this stage in his career. While Dave had never pitched in Little League, he was known to have a tremendous arm and was quite comfortable in throwing a ball from the outfield fence to home plate at the Bayonne Little League. Both had gotten clutch hits during their time in the Little League, and both felt that if the situation required it, they could come up with a hit that would make a difference.

With the boys relaxed and settled in, the game began. Dave threw a couple of strikes to Chuck, who missed one entirely and fouled the other one off. On the third pitch with one of the better balls, Dave threw a high inside strike, and Chuck hit it on the ground in the place where the shortstop normally would have been. There was one out. With the next few pitches, Chuck sought his timing, and Dave sought his velocity. On the next pitch, however, Dave left one of the better balls significantly over the plate and Chuck launched into it with the bat speed and power that sometimes dazzled even Dave. The ball was hit long and far into left-center field. Chuck yelled out, "I think I got all of that one, Dave!"

"Yeah! I think you did," Dave responded. Both boys decided it was a homerun, and the score was 1-nothing.

With the better balls now out of play, it was time to use the balls with the faulty stitches. Dave bore down with these balls, and after getting a come-backer to himself, he was able to entice Chuck to hit an easy pop-up to an imaginary centerfielder. After the first half inning,

Chuck had scored a run, but now it was time for Dave to come to bat. In his first at-bat, Dave knew that Chuck had something special going this day. His fast ball seemed just a bit faster, and although Dave was feeling pretty good about his athletic abilities that day, he found himself having a great deal of difficulty keeping up with the speed of Chuck's fastball. Although he was not able to do any significant hitting through the first third innings, he didn't allow Chuck any more runs. Chuck sent a couple men as far as third but wasn't able to score.

In the fourth, Chuck hit a particularly high drive—a particularly long and high drive—but both the brothers agreed that any capable fielder probably would have caught that ball right at the fence. Later, in the bottom of the fourth, Dave was able to hit the two best balls in foul territory before he got to the two balls with stitch problems later on in his at-bat. With great concentration, he hit the second stitched ball for a clear double when he already had a man on second base. Thus, after an intense rivalry over four innings, the score stood 1-1.

At this point, both of the boys were totally covered with sweat. Each of them was also beginning to feel a slight bit of fatigue. After all, when they weren't pitching or batting, each one was running around the outfield, picking up baseballs that would lie all over the field. In the top of the fifth, after two outs, Chuck really started to attack Dave's pitching. On the first pitch, he ripped a two-out double into the right center-gap. With the next good ball, Chuck launched a liner down the left field line which clearly would have been a double no matter where they played, and so Chuck was now ahead 2-1. As he looked at Dave on the pitching mound, Chuck couldn't help but yell out to him, "Yeah, the end is near buddy; you're collapsing! You just lost it! You have nothing left! I guess the one of us that is the better athlete is taking over."

As he listened to these words, Dave could feel his skin turning red, and his heart turning hard. He had lost to Chuck in the previous week, and he didn't want to lose now. Anybody could get a hit at any time. It didn't mean that he had lost the game, nor did it mean that he had lost his ability.

As his rage grew, Dave bore down on the pitches he was throwing with the stitched balls. The best Chuck was able to do with those stitched balls was to launch a couple of late swinging fouls that were clearly out of play. With his emotions high, Dave picked up the taped ball to make his final pitches. With the heavy weight of the ball and his increased energy, Dave threw the ball as fast as he could with the happy result that he struck Chuck out and ended the inning.

Dave was able to keep Chuck at bay through the eighth inning. In the bottom of the eighth, both boys were tired, and Dave was beginning to feel nausea. Yet, he was not ready to lose to his brother—no, not on this day. With a runner on second and one of the stitched balls being thrown, Dave smashed a sharp shot right down the third base foul line. Although at first Chuck thought the ball was foul, when he looked at it again, he was ready to admit that Dave had indeed hit a double. The score was now 2-2. Unwilling to congratulate his brother for a good hit, Chuck turned to him and said, "You piece of crap, you are the luckiest player who has ever played this game! From what I could see, that was fair by about three inches. Don't worry, baby, that will be the last run you will score on me. It is all over for you, buddy!"

As Dave heard these words, he was not too happy about the attitude of his brother. From Dave's point of view, his brother had seemed to adopt an air of superiority that was not consistent with what was going on in the field. Chuck acted as if he could never lose! Yet here in these games, it was clearly obvious that the outcome of any game was really a matter of luck, not a matter of destiny. As he thought about what his brother had said, Dave started to get angrier and angrier. Who did his brother think he was? What kind of disrespect did his brother have for him?

As he approached the top of the ninth with the score tied, Dave wished to make one point finally and unmistakably clear. Each brother could win the game. Each brother was as good as the other. And Dave this day wanted to prove that he was not only as good as, but better than, his brother could possibly think he was.

As the top of the ninth opened, the temperature on this grassy field in the middle of a Bayonne summer was over ninety degrees. Both players were soaked in sweat. Dave had not only been feeling a bit nauseous, he had also been developing an increasingly painful headache for the last few innings. In fact, in the top of the eighth he had felt a little bit dizzy. He wanted to go for a drink at the water fountain that was two hundred yards away, but both he and Chuck had found out on many occasions that there was a malfunction with the water fountain, and the long trip over there would often be repaid not with water but with disappointment. "*If I can just finish this inning*, Dave thought, "*then*

I will be able to get as long a drink, as good a drink, as satisfying a drink, as I have ever wanted."

Chuck could see that his brother was physically extended, but he was extended too. Yet in the family of these two brothers, to admit any weakness, to ask for any quarter, was to admit that one was not up to snuff. Chuck took some satisfaction in seeing his brother's weakness, but he was not complacent about it. While he too felt some weakness, he knew that there were reserves in the genetics of the two brothers that could enable them to go on—far beyond—what many people they knew could do.

Chuck remembered a time when in Boy Scouts he and his brother in had been able to take a fifteen mile hike in weather that decimated the rest of their troop. While ninety-five degrees had seemed extraordinary for everyone else in the troop, Chuck and Dave felt it a challenge that they could overcome. When help finally arrived for the rest of the scouts, Chuck and Dave had already walked an additional two miles to their destination. Giving into the environment, therefore, was not part of Chuck's or Dave's makeup.

As Chuck got up for the ninth inning with the score tied, a bit of breeze began to blow off Newark Bay and onto the fields of Hudson County Park. Gliding across the sweat of Chuck's body, the slight cool breeze made him feel somewhat renewed in his activities against his brother. It was about quarter to two in the afternoon—the hottest part of the day—but Chuck didn't feel oppressed by the heat. As Dave tossed the first good ball towards Chuck, he ripped a clear single into the right field area. With the next pitch, another clear single emerged. "You've lost it Dave, baby! You've lost what you need to win. It's choke time for you, buddy. It's choke time."

Dave did not appreciate this taunting, so when he took the broken stitched balls, he worked particularly hard to make them curve. His first badly stitched ball led to a grounder which was clearly an out. He couldn't call it a double play because it was a particularly slow grounder, but it was an out nevertheless. The second badly stitched ball also had a negative effect for Chuck, and so now there were two outs with both brothers agreeing that there were probably runners at second and third.

"You ain't got nothing left, Dave," bawled Chuck. "You never had been able to deal with pressure in the clutch! In fact a lot of our friends think you stink when the pressure is on!"

These words really galled Dave. While he knew he had not been a good clutch performer, he knew that he had been pretty good in a few pressure situations. To hear his brother deny some of the best things that he had ever done really bothered him. He vowed he would prove once and for all that he could handle the tough situations.

As he looked at Chuck who had gotten ready for the next pitch, Dave wiped the salty sweat from his eyebrows. He knew he had to strike Chuck out. Another hit might bring in two runs—a lot to make up in his next at-bat. Dave reached down and grabbed the taped ball. He rocked back on his right leg and threw the ball as hard as he could in the direction of the outside of the plate. Chuck seemed a bit slow in getting to the ball, but, he did manage to foul it back on the fence. "Throw that one again, Dave, and I will smack it right down your throat."

After Chuck threw the taped ball back to the mound, Dave considered what he needed to do with his next pitch. Chuck had moved up on the plate in order to reach the outside part more quickly. Dave was not going to give into this; he wasn't going to give Chuck the chance to get a good swing at an outside pitch. He told himself that he would brush the big-mouth off the plate. He thought this was a good time for a little chin music. Summoning all this reserves, Dave threw the taped ball high and inside.

Perhaps Chuck didn't see the ball that clearly. Perhaps Dave had thrown it a bit more inside than he wished. In any event, the taped ball smashed into Chuck's left temple. He dropped instantly on the ground, and Dave froze for a second where he stood. He looked in disbelief at his fallen brother and started shouting, "Get up! Get up! Get up!"

As he approached Chuck, Dave could see no breathing, and a little bit of blood seemed to be coming from Chuck's ear and his nostrils. As he looked around, he saw no one nearby. The only place he could go for help was that mower about five hundred yards off. He began to run in that direction not thinking about how tired he was, not thinking about the heat, and not thinking at all about what he had done.